THE MANY THAT I AM

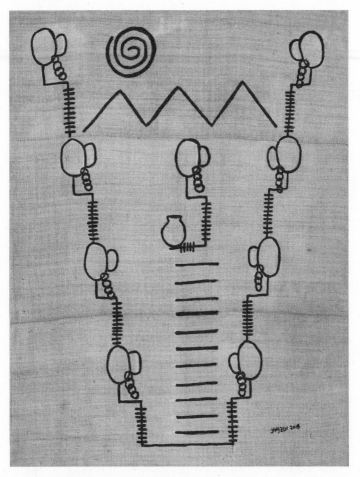

© Iris Yingzen, 2018. Acrylic on hand-woven nettle shawl.

THE MANY THAT I AM

Writings from Nagaland

ANUNGLA ZOE LONGKUMER

Editor

zubaan

ZUBAAN
128 B Shahpur Jat, 1st Floor
New Delhi 110 049
Website: www.zubaanbooks.com
Email: contact@zubaanbooks.com

First published by Zubaan Publishers Pvt. Ltd 2019

Published in association with the Sasakawa Peace Foundation

10 9 8 7 6 5 4 3 2 1

ISBN 978 93 85932 79 3

Zubaan is an independent feminist publishing house based in New Delhi with a strong academic and general list. It was set up as an imprint of India's first feminist publishing house, Kali for Women, and carries forward Kali's tradition of publishing world-quality books to high editorial and production standards. *Zubaan* means tongue, voice, language, speech in Hindustani. Zubaan publishes in the areas of the humanities, social sciences, as well as in fiction, general non-fiction, and books for children and young adults under its Young Zubaan imprint.

Typeset in Baskerville 11/14 by Jojy Philip
Printed and bound by Replika Press Pvt. Ltd, India

Contents

Acknowledgments

For the invitation and the challenge in the first place, I am grateful to Urvashi Butalia, and everyone at Zubaan. Thank you, for your belief and confidence in me.

To all the writers and illustrators whose works make this book, Thank you for your positivity, and trusting me with your work.

To my English teachers and literary guides whom I am blessed to have within such close reach of me: my mother Temsula Ao, and my cousin Narola Changkija, I am indebted to both of you for the invaluable lessons you have taught me in English, and the subtle art of telling. Unstudied as I am in things literary, I never could have done justice to this work without your critical and crucial inputs helping to shape its final outcome. The credit for the edit of *The Many That I Am* goes as much to the two of you.

To all my friends and family who recommended writers and helped me in art direction, Thank you, for being there and being so supportive.

Acknowledgements

Introduction

ANUNGLA ZOE LONGKUMER

Long before I knew the meaning of the word 'displaced',
my life had already been displaced. My great-grandparents
had already been told in their time to abandon all of their
beliefs, for everything they had believed to be true was now
'wrong' or 'sinful' according to the new religion in the land,
brought by the American Baptist Mission who arrived in the
Naga Hills towards the end of the nineteenth century. There
are no written records of what impact this had on the psyche
of my ancestors, but I did meet a tattooed grandmother who
remembered the excitement of the day she had received
her first tattoos, but also how sad she had been on her first
day at the new school in the village; how as a young girl she
had been pointed out by the teacher in front of everybody
for having a 'dirty' face. She had run off to the corner to
rub off the marks from her face, only to realize they were
permanent. She would from then on face condemnation
daily, for wearing her clan tattoos on her face. Some things
of the past still hurt.

At convent school in Shillong, Meghalaya, where I grew up, we were not allowed to speak our mother-tongue and were told to speak English at home. Shillong has always been the hub of education in Northeast India, and quite cosmopolitan ever since the British made it their station in 1864, through its days as the capital of composite Assam since 1937, attaining its own statehood in 1972. But the one event that brought Naga culture up-close for me was the annual Naga Fresher's Day when we watched the Naga student community dance and sing in tribal groups, wearing colourful traditional cloths and jewellery and painted-on tattoos.

The journey back to my roots then began in an indirect way when my mother was awarded a Fulbright fellowship and went to Minnesota in the United States to spend time with the Ojibway people. When she returned, she brought back turtle pendants, feather earrings, dreamcatchers and folklore books. I read each one of the books from cover to cover and tried fashioning out a dreamcatcher myself, feeling a deep sense of connection with my brothers and sisters from another land. My mother was, in turn, inspired by her experience and travelled to Ao villages whenever time and means permitted and this resulted in the book *The Ao-Naga Oral Tradition*, first published in 1999. Finally, I could read stories about my own people written in the English language. What further fuelled my search for connection was my longing for a tattoo. I had so far held back from getting one, firstly out of fear of needles and secondly out of not wanting to get a tattoo from a catalogue, but one day my elder sister who was studying sociology at college handed me a book on the Aos by J.P. Mills. When I found the segment on the Ao tattoo tradition, I knew. *Ao tattoos on my skin? For sure*. Finding Ao tribal tattoos in that book actually helped me come to terms with the reservations I had about the colonists. Recognizing it as a return gift, I was grateful. Later, when I visited Ao villages, I met a tattooed grandmother who drew me to her side and told me, 'Take these (pointing to the tattoos), take them as far away as you can.'

When my ancestors built a cane bridge over the river Dikhu and migrated out of the ancient large settlement of Chungliyimti, they came to be referred to as 'Aor' – those who went away – and to this day we are known as Aor or Ao. Perhaps living up to that name, I too went some distance away from my birthplace, carrying the tattoos, travelling and living elsewhere in the country. Then in 2015 I came to live in Nagaland; and found things had not changed that much from a decade ago when I had come on a short visit: people were still held up by bad roads and power cuts were still a constant. One day while meeting with elder men in a village, the news of women in the fray for the elections to the urban local bodies came up in the conversation and one of the men burst out, 'Men are at the head, and women are below, and it must always remain so!' It hit me then that I was now in a patriarchal society in Nagaland, after growing up in a matrilineal society in Meghalaya, and being exposed to other societies around the world. Then a random person saw the tattoos on me and quoted from the Bible, something to the effect that it was 'a sin to mark thy skin,' and I realized I was now in a Christian state. Afterwards, when I worked on a folklore book project which took me travelling to villages in the interiors, I met a grandfather who only said, 'chapter closed', and being a Christian now, refused to narrate a word of any old story that he knew. I didn't press him, but

3

I could see nothing wrong in wanting to know more about my ancestry, even as we as a people try to move on. I, for one, have found my breathing spaces in the experiences of re-connecting with my roots.

Like for instance when I received a surprise email from Zubaan some months ago asking if I would be interested in compiling and editing works by Naga women writers to be published by them...

Without much ado, I said 'Yes' although to my mind the time frame for holding space as editor of the project seemed short. After word of it rippled out, most of my meetings with the translators and writers and illustrators, as was with the publisher, happened through phone, email and WhatsApp living as they all do in different districts of Nagaland or other states of India or other countries. While on the phone with one of the first contacts I made, she mentioned having done Philosophy in Japanese Studies at university and I thought, 'We're off to a good start!' for I had just received an email from Zubaan saying that this book was in collaboration with the Sasakawa Peace Foundation from Japan. Thanks to them, a space opened up in the cyber world where Naga women writers could take a breather, express themselves, give vent, say their say, in any genre, with the focus on Belonging, or Self, or Identity. Technology, with the relative distance and isolation from the outside world it affords, was in this case a boon, providing conditions conducive for instant communication, reading, and writing. The narratives fell into place on their own, becoming the essence of the book. Set in a man's world, they speak of a woman's journey in words and in pictures worth a thousand more words of their own. Engaging with all the many Naga authors and artists who contributed to this book in such a short time was challenging, most fulfilling, and yet another strong connection to my roots.

I'm hopeful that this first volume of stories by Naga women writers will serve its purpose and many more will follow in the coming years. Nagaland holds many stories in her, each with the need for telling.

The Many That I Am contains an assortment of literary genres like short stories, poems, essays and personal reflections by Naga girls and women. Among the authors, there are quite a few debutantes along with those whose writings have been well-received by the reading public not only in Nagaland but elsewhere in the country and abroad. This perhaps accounts for the uneven qualitative aspects of the book. But it must be noted that the 'idea' of the book is laudable and welcome because one feels that it is an honest attempt to harness the literary potential of the budding writers of a state where there is no tradition of written literature as literacy itself came to them only towards the end of the nineteenth century.

What we have had through the ages is our oral tradition which encompasses everything about ourselves: our history, language, customs, our beliefs and all other aspects of socio-cultural interaction. This is the essence of literature and therefore even the slightest change or loss of any of these details renders that literature weak and incomplete. And it is this incomplete inheritance that we have as our oral literature today. But one has to accept the fact that the pristine past cannot be restored to its original status, nor should it be attempted.

It is therefore understandable that 'literature' written by Nagas is a relatively recent phenomenon and not too vast in terms of quantity. But what it lacks in quantity is compensated by its quality and the impact it has had on readers and critics alike nationwide and internationally. Not only that, many universities in the country have included these writers' works in their syllabi and quite a few scholars from universities like Jawaharlal Nehru University, the Northeastern Hill University, Burdwan, Sikkim, NU and even Tirupati are writing their M.Phil and PhD theses on the works of some Naga writers.

In the last decade or two, we have seen a host of Naga writers venturing into writing literature of a different kind in English which is inevitable because there is no common Naga language. What is quite interesting in many of these writings is that the elements of the oral tradition have provided the main inspiration. Beginning from the first story *Where the Hills Grow Houses*, many of the narratives in this book display the bond between the past and the present. Incidentally, this story also highlights the obvious dichotomy between development and environment. Such reflections are evident in many of the stories and poems in the first section of the book.

The remarkable feat in transforming the past by coalescing it with our present circumstances bears ample testimony to the inherent creativity of our young writers. In many of these writings one also finds the important theme of introspection, looking at ourselves in a more critical way. Instead of 'others' depicting a somewhat superficial image of the Nagas, it is Naga writers who are now espousing the need for honest probity into our inner selves in order to correct our past mistakes by creating a livable present. Therefore, we see that if oral sources inspire the literary works, current affairs and politics also resonate from many of the pieces included in this collection.

A prominent theme that runs through this book is the feminine/feminist voice which questions the continued dominance of the male over the female and the constant helplessness endured by women in the intransigent patriarchal society of the Nagas. *My Mother's Daughter* is a case in point. Even the poem, *Konyak Folk Song* is a poignant cry against this kind of gender-based discrimination.

Some of the non-poetic, non-fictional writings in this collection, may perhaps be termed, 'confessional' as they come from the questionings of the generation caught between the violent past and the increasingly vacuous and corrupt present in search of answers. There is another notable element in these writings which highlights the very pronounced gender-divide in Naga society. *I Wish You Were A Man* is that kind of a poem. Another concern seems to be the urban-rural divide brought on by the new dispensation and class-divide in society, rampant corruption, appeasement and bribery destroying the system.

The present collection is the proof that Nagas are beginning to examine and write about their rootedness to their origins with new perspectives and are scrutinizing their present circumstances with sincere introspection. The inclusion of these writings to the nascent written literature by Nagas has been prompted by the 'potential' displayed in the 'first offerings' of many of the contributors. Though they mostly write about the present, glimpses of the past are incorporated in subtle ways to create a kind of fusion. The resultant catalytic framework then affords them the means to explore the relevance of past values on the complexities of their social positioning in the contemporary context. In such a symbiotic process, recollection of the past, inclusion, inversion and re-interpretation of orality into the written text has enabled quite a few Naga writers to engage in a literary activity which may one day be acknowledged as the genesis of a new literature from Nagaland.

Cycle of Life

MOASO AIER

Oil on canvas.

Where the Hills Grow Houses

EMISENLA JAMIR

Every morning, for the last thirty years, Mangyang would wake up at four o'clock. He would go into the kitchen, fill up a large aluminium mug with water, and set it to boil on the ancient stove. As he waited for the water to boil up, he would squat by the hearth and pull out firewood from the stack kept neatly on the *tsukden*. Then, placing the wood strategically in the fireplace exactly like his mother used to do some forty odd years ago, he would light a crumpled page of an old newspaper, shove it underneath the dry wood and watch as the fire caught. He would then haul himself up and make tea for everybody in the house, pouring a cup for himself. By then, a cheerful fire would be roaring in the hearth and Mangyang would welcome his tea like an old friend.

This particularly fine March morning was no exception. He savoured this time of the day, listening to the birdsong and feeling the soft rays of the rising sun as it gently enveloped the house. It was just him, his tea and the soft glow of dawn.

Having drunk up his first cup of tea, he poured himself a second and went outside. In front of the house was a tiny compound barely large enough to be able to stretch one's legs and hang up laundry. Barbed wire circled the house demarcating the boundary that ended at the gate to the extreme right.

Just below his house, was a small plot of land belonging to Kevi. Kevi's house stood to the left, adjacent to the empty plot. Mangyang often saw Aja, Kevi's wife, pottering around the tiny plot, watering herbs and planting flowers haphazardly, happily humming an old tune she had learnt in the great gospel revival of 1973.

Standing at the edge of the compound, Mangyang stretched his back languidly, placing his free hand on the iron pipe positioned atop two bamboo poles on which his wife hung their laundry. He loved watching the sunrise with its brilliant glow of different reds filling up the sky. He closed his eyes, lifting his head up, feeling the warmth seep through his body and into his bones. He could feel the heat of the sun coursing through his blood and imagined it deepening its colour. Sipping his tea contentedly, Mangyang surveyed the land that stretched out in front. Half of Kohima lay before him, and as he watched the sunlight slowly creep across the expanse and alight on the tin roofs, a shadow crossed his serene face. The hills are growing houses, he thought. He remembered a time when the hills had been covered with trees. Then, only small government quarters built in neat rows and some private residences dotted the hillsides. Now, huge concrete buildings loomed menacingly over the small quarters hiding them from view. He fancied he heard the hills groaning with the weight of all that concrete. He tried

11

to remove the grim image of the hills collapsing beneath the weight of the buildings as he finished having his tea.

When he went inside for his third cup, his wife was already in the kitchen pouring out some tea herself. Cradling the warm mug in her hands, she took her seat by the fireplace and began telling him about her latest dream. He wondered why she bothered with dreams when there were more important things to be discussed. Still, he listened and nodded as he had done so for the past thirty years.

He looked at her and tried to remember why he had married her. He used to love her, or at least he thought he did. Lines had now formed on her forehead and her skin was all dried up. There were uneven patches on her cheeks which she tried to hide unsuccessfully with what women called 'foundation'. He thought back on their wedding day and tried to remember how she looked then, but all he could see was a white veil over her aged face. He shook his head, waving away imaginary flies and cleared his throat, nodding sagely as she described a particular scene. 'And not just one fish! Hundreds of them, flapping their helpless fins, gasping for air! I wonder what that could mean,' she mused.

His eyes wandered around the kitchen and landed on the rickety table. I'll mend it one of these days, he thought to himself. 'I know,' he half-heard his wife say, 'I'll ask Oya Asang. Her interpretations always prove correct.' He heard his voice from far away agreeing with her.

Mangyang had recently retired from his government job as the Superintendent in the department of Rural Development and kept himself occupied with mending things around the house. He tried not to dwell on the future. He barely had a future. He was way past his prime and now the years following his retirement loomed like a dark chasm in front of him. The thought of stepping into that void scared him. But what truly frightened him was the prospect of his wife's retirement. The transition had happened so slowly that it surprised him. Not only did he not know his own wife, he barely seemed to know the person he had become. There were, of course, the habitual everyday predictions that any married couple could make: mood swings, that particular tone of her voice, all the varied facets that seem to dwell within an individual. But it ended there. He did not want to go beyond that, did not want to understand his wife nor himself anymore. People got wiser as they grew older, more in tune with other people. Not him. He just wanted to stay at home quietly and do the things that he was supposed to do – like drink tea and watch television. It was not that he wished her dead. He just didn't want to see her all the time. To be alone with her for the rest of his retired life filled him with a dread he could barely articulate.

His eldest daughter ran a boutique in Dimapur where she was settled with her husband. His youngest was in Delhi, working at a call centre. He still did not understand why she would want to work all through the night talking to strangers when she could be home, happily married to an honest and hard working man. He had never really been close to his children. He was disappointed that he had no sons to whom he could impart words of wisdom as his father had done to him. Sometimes when he looked over at Kevi's house, he would hear the man and his three sons laughing together. Occasionally, they raised their voices over heated arguments but that only seemed to add to Mangyang's loneliness. He resented his wife a little, even though he knew she was not to be blamed. He looked around the kitchen again and saw the mug he had used in college hanging by a hook on the blackened wall. He rose from and went into the sitting room and switched on the television to watch the morning news, only half aware of his wife peeling potatoes for their morning meal.

By noon, his wife had already left for her office and he was all alone. It was a hot afternoon and he did not feel like repairing the table. He went outside hoping to see Aja. He looked down and sure enough there she was, busy lining up flowerpots neatly by the doorway of her house.

'Cleaning flower pots, are you?' he asked her.

Aja looked up in surprise, 'Oh, hello! I didn't see you there. I'm just relocating these pots. Did my husband not tell you?' she glanced up at Mangyang, and bent down, shifting pots around. Then standing up and wiping away the sweat trickling down her brow with the edge of her sleeve she said, 'We finally sold the land.'

She saw Mangyang looking down at her quizzically, 'Sold what land?'

'This little plot, right here,' she said.

Mangyang saw Aja's dusty fingers point at the empty plot which he had hoped would one day be his. 'But why?' he asked, numerous other questions popping up in his mind.

'Oh, you know,' Aja answered him unhurriedly. 'What with Kohima being the capital and all, everybody seems to be grabbing land these days. Any tiny plot will do for them. So, apparently, Ato will be retiring in a few years' time and he wants a place of his own. He's a good friend of Kevi's, and since we need the money for our sons' education, we thought it over and finally agreed to sell it to him.'

Mangyang felt various emotions churning up inside him. He finally grabbed hold of one and held on to it. Vexed. He was extremely vexed. Wasn't *he* a good friend? Why! He had practically badgered and begged them to sell him that piece of land. Even on those nights when they had got together to drink *phika cha* he had pestered them to sell it to him. Land prices had skyrocketed due to the increase in demand and he had hoped to settle down on a piece of land that was his own by the time he retired. But for all his hopes, Mangyang had finally accepted defeat and grudgingly bought a plot of land in Dimapur instead. Although this land was bigger and comparatively cheaper, he felt no satisfaction with the bargain. His heart lay in Kohima and he considered his present emotional churnings as very valid.

Sensing Mangyang's discomfort Aja tried to pacify him, 'We had no choice. We never thought of selling it, but with three children studying outside, you know how it is.'

Mangyang forced himself to smile, 'Of course, I understand. It's not easy raising children outside Nagaland.' Then feigning a shocked expression, he said, 'Oh how stupid of me! I completely forgot I left the milk boiling on the stove!' He hastily entered his house and shut the door behind him. He blinked away the bright lights that swam before his eyes as they adjusted to the sudden darkness indoors.

He stood there clenching and unclenching his fists. He wanted to do something, but he did not know what. He paced around the house, arranging and rearranging things in the rooms. He suddenly remembered the milk on the stove and rushed into the kitchen. Only, there was no milk on the stove. He had forgotten that he had lied to excuse himself from a volatile situation. A minute longer outside and he would have burst out in anger. His hands shook. He could no longer be merely vexed, he could only allow his pent-up emotions to run riot. For nearly five years, he had begged and badgered them to sell him the land and now! They had the nerve to throw it away to somebody they barely even knew! In three years his wife would retire, and they would have to vacate these government quarters. Years of emotions held within the house would give way to new people and their emotions. New love, new hate and new despair would fill up the house erasing all the old emotions. And where would they be then? Far away in a land he barely even cared about!

Kohima reminded him of home. The transition from his village to the state capital had been made easier because of the landscape. The hills reminded him of where he had grown up and the green trees and the cool air had made him feel comfortable and at home. He loved his village, but it had held no possibilities and Kohima with its endless possibilities and the attractive verdant expanse had beckoned him, and he had not regretted his decision to move here. Regrets. His only regret was not having saved enough money to buy a piece of land for himself here. And now, it was too late.

Mangyang could not sleep that night. His wife thought he looked listless, but then he was always listless. She thought he might be coming down with a cold and gave him a Disprin tablet, just in case. He dutifully swallowed the medicine with a glass of cold water. The water tasted fresh and clean. He hated the water in Dimapur. Even the air there smelled funny. It stank of concrete and cow shit and sweat. He watched the NDTV channel and slept off quite fitfully on the sofa. He woke up suddenly at 3 a.m. He must have switched off the television at some point. He sat up, wide awake, not able to go back to sleep. At exactly four o' clock, he got up and went into the kitchen to make tea.

Mangyang went about his daily routine, except now there was something missing. Perhaps it was the way he carried himself, perhaps it was his reticence, but no one noticed that anything was amiss except Aja. Ever since the day he had received the news, he had been behaving a little out of sorts. He was a quiet man, but he seemed quieter still. Early in the mornings while she tended her flowers, she started to catch him looking longingly at the empty plot. She tried to engage him in conversation, but he would retort abruptly and go into his house. Aja started worrying about Mangyang's changed demeanour, but Kevi brushed aside her fears as 'female nonsense'.

This habit of scrutinizing the land finally stopped the day the workers came to lay down the foundation. Mangyang ceased socialising altogether and went to the bazaar only when absolutely necessary. His wife kept insisting that he go and see a doctor, but he just blamed his blood pressure on his listlessness and waved off her fears.

The new owner, Ato, started coming to his house often to ask for small favours. Mangyang tried to be gracious, but it took all of his efforts to be congenial towards the person who, he felt, had stolen his land. Months passed and the building slowly started taking shape. The loud construction noises irritated Mangyang and he would often storm out and shout at the workers for no apparent reason. And when no one was looking, he would spit on the land below his house. Sensing his mood, Ato soon stopped asking for favours.

In the evenings, Mangyang would go outside and listen

to the workers still hammering away. They were building it all wrong, he said to himself. The building rose up and levelled with his house. The first thing he now saw in the morning when he stepped outside was the grey building. No longer could he see the sunrise or the sunset. The immutable blankness of the grey building cast a shadow over his house, over himself, and his soul.

As the days passed, Mangyang's wife grew more and more worried. One day, she came home from office and found her husband was missing. She looked everywhere for him and finally found him sitting on the tin roof solemnly watching the sunset. He told her he had washed his clothes and laid them out on the roof and was waiting for them to dry. She did not believe him but said nothing. She was in a hurry to go down to Dimapur. Her daughter was in the hospital about to give birth. There seemed to be no point in asking her husband to accompany her. She was worried about him, but her daughter needed her attention more. And besides, she thought, he might be better off on his own for a few days. By the time Mangyang climbed down from the roof, his wife had already packed up and was ready to leave. He expressed no concern or excitement when she told him that their daughter had gone into labour. Lately, she had begun to wonder who her husband was. She asked him to take care of himself and to call her if anything happened. 'I will,' was all he said as she hurriedly handed her bags to the driver waiting for her.

Mangyang watched his wife's receding figure until she disappeared from view. He latched the gate and picking up a plastic chair from the kitchen sat outside watching the workers constructing the building. He heard loud laughter coming from down below. He recognised the voices of Ato and Kevi and he clenched his hands into tight fists. 'Thief!' he muttered. He looked up at the grey soulless building and kept repeating, 'They are building it all wrong…they are building it all wrong…'

Lying down in bed that night Mangyang listened to the swishing sounds of tall bamboos as they swayed in the howling wind outside. The sounds brought back a sensation he had long forgotten and he was comforted by its familiarity. He slept soundly and woke up precisely at four o'clock. As usual, he drank his cup of tea and went outside. He saw no sunrise, felt no warmth coursing through his body. The remnants of his dream evaporated and he looked up angrily at the half-built structure that seemed to sap the life out of him. He checked the skin on his hands and arms. It looked pale and grey. He heard a small sound and turned around to see Ato walk in through the open gate.

'Good morning!' Ato greeted him.

'Good morning', Mangyang replied curtly. *Thief!* he spat inside his head.

Ato handed him a plastic bag. 'I brought you something,' he said jovially. The bag was smeared in blood. Mangyang made no move to accept it. 'Here,' Ato insisted. 'It's just some pork. A friend of mine butchered a local pig and I got some for you and Kevi.'

Mangyang forced himself to smile as he reluctantly accepted the bag. 'Thank you. You really shouldn't have.'

'It's no problem. What are neighbours for, right?' Ato grinned, 'I'll be off then. I need to go buy some more stuff for the house. These lazy *mistris* are afraid to venture out because their inner-line permits have expired.'

Mangyang nodded and managed another smile. 'Thank you again,' he forced the words out of his mouth. Ato turned and walked away and was at the gate when he heard Mangyang say something which sounded to his ears like 'Thief!'

He paused a moment and then walked back slowly towards Mangyang. The man was lost in his thoughts and did not hear him return. He stood looking up at the building clutching the blood splattered polythene bag in his hands muttering to himself, 'Stupid thief! Neighbourly indeed! What does he think of himself! Stealing what was mine!'

'Thief? Am I a thief then?' Ato spoke up. 'Is this what I get for trying to be friends?'

The man turned to stare at Ato and then looked at the building and then faced Ato again with dead eyes. 'Yes,' he said loudly. 'You are a miserable thief! You march in here with your fake smile and hand me this measly stinking piece of pork and you think it will make things right between us?' he shouted.

'Hey! I paid good money for this land!' Ato said. 'It's not yours. It never was in the first place. What's the matter with you?'

'Matter with me? What is the matter with *you*? Why would you go about stealing what was mine, you miserable thief!'

'Why are you picking on me? I think you should go and speak with Kevi about this. It's not my problem. Stop involving me in your insane imaginings!'

'Leave Kevi out of this! You good-for-nothing thief!'

Ato became rigid with anger. 'That's enough!' he said. 'One more word and I promise you I'll not be responsible for my actions!'

'I will not be responsible for my actions!' the man mimicked him.

Ato was not an unreasonable man but his patience had been tried and tested by this man for too long now. And so, as promised, he raised his big fist and punched Mangyang on his left cheek. The man staggered back in shock but quickly regained his composure. Clutching the polythene bag tightly in his hand, he swung it hard at Ato hitting him on the head. As Ato lay dazed on the ground, Mangyang twisted the polythene bag around his hands tightly and using it as a club swung it over and over again and with every contact it made with Ato's head, he kept saying, 'Thief! Thief! Thief!'

A mixture of pig and human blood now covered both his hands. By the time he stopped swinging his arm, Ato's face was all swollen up and hardly recognisable. Mangyang looked at the body and then at the building. His blood splattered face widened into a smile as he felt imaginary sun rays coursing through his body. He finally let go of the polythene bag and deep lines were etched around his hand where the plastic was wrapped too tightly. Their shouts had alerted the neighbourhood and people were stirring, trying to ascertain the location of all the noise.

Mangyang stood up and walked out of his gate, his bloodied hands hanging limply by his side. When Ato's body was finally discovered, Mangyang had long disappeared from the neighbourhood. There was no necessity to notify the police however; a young constable had found an old man sitting in a corner outside the South Police station. He listened to the ramblings of the deranged man, nodding gently as he cautiously manoeuvred the handcuffs around his bloodied hands. He tried to hurry the old man in through the gates before the mob could gather to demand blood.

Mangyang smiled at the constable leading him inside the police station. 'You understand why I had to do it now, don't you, son?' he asked. 'He stole my sunlight. You see, he stole my sunlight.'

Viyili

(Sumi-Naga folk song)

Translated by
AHIKALI SWU

Woe is me! Viyili
The child of Lhoupu.
Oh, like a child pampered upon
I was lavished so.
Oh! So doted upon was I
Among folks I mingled not,
Their wood I carried not.*

Oh! If folks were of flowers,
Monsoon clusters they were,
The old, the young alike
Plucked them all away.
Oh! If I were of flowers
A precious bloom I was,
Perched on high rocky cliffs,

Plucked away by none.
Oh! If folks were of fishes,
Along the shores, they were,
The old, the young alike
Could catch them all away.
Oh! If I were of fishes,
Upon the deepest, I was,

Only the skilled of divers
Could catch upon me so.

My trophy head bestow
Onto Khuvushe's father
Upon the great one
Is my prideful place,
My heart's desire too.
On equal terms with folks
Never treat me so,
A restless soul,
Then I will be.
Alas! Father of mine,
This world is fading away
My brothers, let them walk me
Till path of death I reach.**

Legend has it that Viyili was a beautiful young girl adored by all, who was killed and beheaded during a tribal feud. Necromany or the practice of communicating with the spirits of the dead through a medium was normally practised by our forefathers. This was usually done in cases of untimely deaths to appease the souls of the victims.

* One of the main chores of youngsters was collecting firewood and water.
** Most animist Nagas believed that upon death, the spirit usually went upon a mount (believed to be Wokha mountain), and the path leading to the top was referred to as the 'path of death' (Kithila). Source: Sukhevi Chiso, Sutemi village, Nagaland. First published in *A Glimpse of Long Ago* (HPH, 2014), p. 21.

Cut Off

VISHÜ RITA KROCHA

Every male child in the village followed in his father's footsteps and Tasu had been no exception. He was born in 1905 in Zhavame village which lies in remote south-east Nagaland. Tasu grew up in a time when a good life was quantified by the number of paddy barns you could fill. His parents had several of these *thu bao* lined up neatly in the corridor of their big thatched house. These large grain baskets stood beside the wooden house pillars which, like the walls, were decorated with the skulls of men and women whose heads had been brought back as trophies by the village warriors. As the village chief, Tasu's father enjoyed the privilege of adorning his house with these skulls.

While he was still a little boy, Tasu's father sat him down on the grassy compound in front of their house and showed him his spear. Holding the staff horizontally, his father told him how he had made it with his own hands using only his machete. Turning the spear about carefully, his father pointed to the tufts of red hair on the wood and said that he himself had bound the hair from an enemy head after he had dyed the strands with the juice of a plant growing in the jungles nearby. The metal tip of the spearhead glinted in the sunlight. Then his father sprang to his feet and yelled a war cry and attacked the air with the spear.

'This is how warriors fight!' he said and, reaching behind him, drew out his machete from its holder at his waist and cut the air in front of him several times with its sharp edge.

Then his father sat beside him again and showed him the spear once more, saying it was his most trusted ally for it had never once failed him. Every male in the village learnt to fight and defend the village. They took the heads of the enemy. This was tradition.

The little boy asked, 'Father, do they take the heads of mothers and children?'

'No, not little children,' his father had replied straightaway. 'But son, remember the enemy will carry off little ones like you, which is why we have village guards keeping watch. And our village gate is always shut after sunset, to prevent enemies from entering our territory.'

The village women did their fieldwork, foraged for food in the jungle, collected wood and fetched water, pounded rice and millet, tended plants and vegetables in the garden, cooked the meals and cared for the children and the elders, and besides other domestic chores, wove cloths, reared pigs, and raised chickens. Seventeen moons passed and then one day Tasu got a big surprise when his father summoned him to a formal meeting and solemnly said, 'Son, it is now your turn. This spear is yours now. You are ready to become a warrior.'

A big lump formed in Tasu's throat and he could not speak a word, but bowing his head, he accepted the spear. He knew how precious it was and what it meant to his father. But he was unsure if he could use it as well. However, his father died soon after, and in great sorrow, Tasu made a vow to keep his memory alive, and from then on, to be on the warpath was his only goal in life.

But by the late 1920s, Christianity was gaining a stronghold in the land of the Nagas. Preachers began coming to Zhavame village, and Tasu, with the rest of the villagers, heard their words. Within a year, he converted to the new religion. Villages which had once fought each other began making peace agreements, and the celebrations they organized went on for days on end with a lot of feasting and cultural shows. During these regular celebrations, people would tell stories and one story in particular started doing the rounds:

A warrior infiltrated an enemy village and cut off the heads of a man and a woman. As he was about to flee with the prized heads he saw two small boys cowering between the woodshed and the kitchen wall. They looked so helpless that the warrior decided to take them home with him. Along the way, the elder of the two boys began to trouble him, kicking his sides, pulling the lock of hair at the back of his head and biting and scratching his neck and shoulders. Annoyed, the man abandoned the elder boy and reached home with only the younger one whom he raised as one of his own.

Eventually, a peaceful alliance was formed between the former hostile villages and people from both sides entertained each other. The singing and dancing and feasting went on for days on end. The boy who had been carried away from his village was now a fine young man. It was a popular belief that if a man came back to his place of birth and took part in the feast, he would die. Despite this, the young man went to his village anyway and when everybody sat down to feast, he joined in eating and drinking heartily.

When Tasu heard the story of the young man, it affected him in a way he couldn't explain. But this was around the time that his nightmares had begun. He would see shadows of men and women in his dreams, surrounding him, their mouths open in silent condemnation. After such dreams, Tasu would wake up in the middle of many a night in a cold sweat.

But the seasons turned and the years rolled by and to his relief, his nightmares began occurring less and less often. He began finding contentment in the peaceful life. He got married and the birth of his son drove away all remaining memories of the past life from his mind. He named the boy Kavikha, *the best*, and began to see a whole new world through him. As the boy grew up, Tasu began telling him stories of his people. He found that after each telling, he felt more and more at peace. And his little boy, much like Tasu had been as a child, listened attentively, and always asked for one more when one story ended. One evening, as the rain pelted the ground outside their house, Tasu re-told what his father had told him when he was this tender age:

> We, we are the enchanted people. We were the first ones on this land. Right at the very beginning, our forefathers conquered the enchanted lake that lay in the heart of the village. They heated up big rocks over open fires and threw them, red-hot, into the waters of the lake, and that's how the evil spell was broken. Then our forefathers said, 'We are the lucky ones, we are the people with charm' and so from then on, that's who we are, we are the enchanted people. After

breaking the spell of the lake, our forefathers transformed the lake into fertile paddy fields. It's that large area right there in the middle of the village which we work in year by year. That is our story.'

Along with Christianity came education. However, education had not yet reached Tasu's village, instead people were sending their sons to study in schools outside Nagaland. Kavikha was twelve when Tasu sent him to a school in Assam to get an education. His son proved to be diligent in his studies and enjoyed the experience of outside cultures. Tasu's face beamed with happiness and pride when Kavikha returned as the first matriculate from the village several years later. But, his proudest moment came a few years after that when his son became the first graduate from the village.

Subsequently, Kavikha secured a good government job. His marriage followed and then came three beautiful children, Tasu's beloved grandchildren. Two of them then went on to make Tasu a great-grandfather. Only Chavi, his youngest granddaughter, now lived at home with her parents.

Kavikha served many years in government service and when he retired from his post, it was only natural that he should stand for the state general elections. Everyone in the village supported him. The villages in their area had been neglected for too long now. They needed proper representation in the state assembly. For Kavikha, it was a bold step to take, for he was from a minority village where people spoke their own dialect and were looked down on by the other bigger villages. He knew it would be a tough battle because the rest of the constituency was comfortable with the leadership of the current elected member. When he consulted his father, Tasu reassured him, 'My son, you have all my blessings. I know you will succeed in what you have undertaken.'

With everybody's blessings, Kavikha won a landslide victory. The five years of his term sped by in rounds of meetings and signing papers, travelling around the districts and attending various functions. Through it all, he tried his best to fulfil many of the basic needs of the villages in his area and things had been fine, up until now when it was time for the next round of elections. Some party workers from the village had become unsatisfied with their end of the bargain and had joined the opposition party supported by the other villages. Trouble was brewing.

10 January 2000, Phek District, Nagaland.

> *'Oh! People of the Enchanted Land, let us be on our way!*
> *Men, young and old, you must all join!'*

These words echoed through Zhavame village on the misty mountaintop. In any other circumstance, these same words would have sounded melodious, but not right now. Two village boys returning from Kohima had brought back news that there was a big movement going on in the area and everyone was alarmed. According to the two, busloads of men from the neighboring villages were headed toward their village, armed with guns, spears, and machetes. This day was exactly a month before voting day.

31

Hearing the clarion call, all the able-bodied men in the village moved quickly. Only the women, children, and the elderly remained sitting by the fireside in their kitchens, many of them muttering prayers. Tasu, who was now the oldest in the village at ninety-five, sat by his fireplace, suddenly disoriented by the pain in his head and the cold fear in his heart brought on by the alarm call. Kavikha was away in the state capital. Tasu wished his son could hear him say: 'We have managed to survive and prosper only because of our unity. We must never ever break it!'

Outside, the men were leaving the village in groups, armed with all the weapons they could get hold of, headed to gather at the playground a distance away. Access to the village from the highway was through this open ground. Every male held a machete, or a spear or a knife. Some of the younger ones looked around for stones and started collecting them in a big heap. The village elders conferred together and a few of them ventured out to the main road to ascertain where the buses had reached. A group of young men from the village suddenly appeared as if from out of nowhere with a stranger in their custody; the stranger was one of those young underground cadres who called themselves 'freedom fighters for the Naga cause.'

'Is this underground fellow associated with the opposition? Maybe they sent him to spy on us!'

The young men were incensed.

The village elders who had gone out to the road came back and one of them stood on the fender of a Bolero and addressed the men who were armed and ready to defend their village with their lives. The elder announced that no man was to raise his hand; they were all to stand their ground in peace. But, if the opposition party attacked and they were compelled to defend their village, then they were to fight back without fear, even if they were outnumbered.

Then all the men started marching toward the main road shouting angrily: 'Who do they think they are? What have we done to upset them? If they cannot win an election by peaceful means then their candidate does not deserve to be elected!' And with every step they took, they heard angry voices from the advancing buses coming closer.

Gloom hung over the village. Tasu sat in his kitchen wondering how swiftly life can change. It was hours since the men had left the village. At least he had the company of his granddaughter Chavi who had come to help campaign for her father. She was folding a stack of her father's campaign flyers on the low table by the fire when they heard the next door neighbour call out to her. Chavi hurried out of the back door and hurried back in. She told her grandfather that the womenfolk were getting worried and that the president of the village women's association was summoning them for a meeting. She tried to coax her grandfather to lie down and rest but he refused, so she put more firewood into the hearth and left for the meeting. Chavi came back within minutes and told her grandfather that the women were going to the playground and started to get ready to leave. 'We must go and offer peace. We cannot afford to let violence take over our lives again,' she quoted the president as saying. Tasu tried to tell Chavi not to go but no words came out. He could only helplessly look at her when she stacked some firewood within his reach and asked him to lie down and try and get some rest. From the doorway, Chavi looked back at her grandfather sitting hunched by the fireside.

'Grandpa, try and get some rest,' she said again, and when her grandfather continued to stare into the fire, she sighed and stepped outside.

With instructions to the young girls to look after the babies and children, all the women left the village and only the very elderly and the very young now remained.

It was all fresh in Tasu's mind as if everything had just happened. He stepped into his house exhausted, after beating the log-drum all night to celebrate his success in the headhunt. Seeing him enter, his wife silently took hot water from the big pot sitting on the three hearthstones and mixed it with some cold spring water in a wooden trough. Rinsing a clean cloth in the hot water, she gently washed off all the blood and grime from his body. Afterwards, they sat side by side in front of the warm fire, comfortable in their silence. Then the image of a woman's long hair caught in a man's grip flashed in his mind and Tasu moaned in pain. He remembered the story of a skull hanging on one of the big wooden pillars in the house, a woman's head, seized by her long hair, cut off, brought home to the village chief. He remembered how he ran home scared for his mother's safety after hearing that story from the older boys in the playground. An image of blood on the blade of a dao and then Chavi's smiling face flashed and Tasu moaned in pain again. He started shivering, feeling a chill even though he was right beside a crackling fire.

Then, Tasu heard a faint sound. He got up and shuffled over to the window. It was close to midnight now. It had been an agonizing wait for him and he was tired. He heard faint sounds of singing and saw flickering lights of the bamboo torches from the direction of the playground. Heart beating fast, he gripped the window frame. Then he heard the lively singing of women growing louder and louder as they passed through the village gates and entered the village. A big wave of relief washed over him. His breathing became easier. When his granddaughter stepped into the kitchen, Tasu turned to her and smiled.

Chavi led her grandfather back to the fireplace and sitting beside him, told him everything: how they had found the men shouting and screaming most savagely, how they were pelting stones, some of them smashing up a parked bus and some others setting fire to old tyres. The acrid black smoke billowing in the air had choked their throats and stung their eyes, but still, the women had walked in a long line toward the men without breaking their stride. The would-be warriors on both sides ceased their fighting when they saw the women. They dropped the stones, lowered their machetes and spears, and became silent. Chavi told her grandfather how afraid she had been, and how brave the women leaders were, talking patiently with the men. Tasu looked at her, draped in her white *rumini* and shawl, and thought she looked like an angel.

Later, when he finally went to bed, he stretched out gratefully and smiled thinking, 'How different the story is when women are around.'

Untitled

LICCA KIHO

Pencil and sketchpen on paper.

Retold by Grandma – Yarla's Tattoos

SIRAWON TULISEN KHATING

Home for me was Shillong, till I went to boarding school where I lived with people from around the world. Learning about their cultures, I became more curious about my own. After college, I finally took on the project of documenting my 'home'. My Azao is now ninety-five years old and the only grandparent alive. She is Ao-Naga and always has stories to share, and sometimes even a song to sing. Her memory is so amazing that even now she remembers names and other minute details very clearly, often pulling out a map or book from her library to show where events took place. Together with my mom, we recorded stories retold by Azao.

And one of the stories that I'll always remember is the story of Yarla's tattoos and how she got them. Azao told this story to me and my mom one evening as we sat by the fireplace after dinner. She closed her eyes and recalled the story of two sisters and the invention of tattooing.

She said…

Noksangmenla and Yarla were very smart and intelligent sisters from the Ozükumer clan. Ozü means bird, but that is another story.

Anyway, as it was in the tradition for young girls back then, Yarla was sent to live in the girl's dormitory in the village, where she would be taught the necessary domestic skills. Now, the other girls from well-to-do families wore necklaces, bangles and other jewellery. But, Yarla wore only a shell on a string as a necklace. So, the other girls teased and bullied her by calling her *chepralikla*. Yarla was sad that the matron of the dormitory allowed the bullying to continue. When she came home for a few days, she told her elder sister Noksangmenla about the bullying. Her sister replied, 'Don't worry little one, one day I will give you some beautiful jewels to wear.'

One afternoon, the sisters went to collect firewood and having completed the task, they sat down to rest on a fallen log. Yarla rested her hand on the log, which happened to be of the *Ngupde* tree, and when she absentmindedly placed her hand on her thigh, she realized that the sap from the log had stained her palm and left a beautiful pattern on the skin of her thigh.

Intrigued, Yarla drew her sister's attention to this beautiful pattern and Noksangmenla immediately exclaimed, 'How beautiful!' Then in the next breath she said, 'I have an idea, come on, help me.'

Slowly and carefully, they collected the sap from the log. At home, Noksangmenla mixed the sap with some soot from the fireplace and heated the mixture to create a dye. She collected some thorns of the cane vine and called her sister into a small inner room. Yarla had grown increasingly puzzled by her sister's activities, but she trusted her, so she did as she was told. She sat quietly while Noksangmenla drew nice patterns on her upper chest, arms, legs, neck and chin with a thin piece of wood dipped in the dye.

Next, Noksangmenla warned Yarla that she was now going to do something that would cause her some pain but it would result in something beautiful. So, Yarla took a deep breath and exhaled, and braced herself while Noksangmenla bound together the thorns of cane with thin strings of plant fibre. Then the thorns were bound to a short stick. Then, she placed the dye-stained tips of the thorns against Yarla's skin and began to tap away. And with every tap, Yarla's skin was punctured and the dye was driven further in. Yarla couldn't help crying out in pain and some neighbours hearing her cries came to inquire, but Noksangmenla sent them away saying her sister had a stomach ache.

After a few days, when Yarla's sores had healed and she stepped out of her house, the villagers were stunned by the intricate patterns on her skin. She looked so beautiful, and everyone, including the matron and the girls from the dormitory, loved the tattoos and longed for such patterns on themselves.

From then on, Azao explained, tattooing became an art. Everyone was allowed to have tattoos, except the *alar*. Azao's mother had tattoos, but she herself does not because by the time she was born, her parents had converted to Christianity.

Taking time out to listen or share stories isn't something families do anymore. In paying more attention to stories and documenting daily life I can hopefully pass them on to coming generations. As a visual artist, this story opens a door in understanding the vast history of how design plays such an important role in creating identity. Noksangmenla's ingenuity and resourcefulness speaks of Nagas and their connection with the land and the genius to use it. It is this that propels me to re-think, imagine and create.

Old Man's Story

JUNGMAYANGLA LONGKUMER

Sanen thought about his friends enjoying their winter holidays in Dimapur while here he was, mucking about with an old man in the village. Sanen had just turned nineteen, a lanky boy with a nice tea-coloured complexion and a massive head of coarse hair that seemed to have a life of its own. He had been brought up to be responsible and obedient, and as the sole heir in his family, it had been drummed into his head that his family depended on him. He had been well-trained by his mother in doing all sorts of chores around the house too. So, when Sanen had been told that his maternal grandfather, Awo Tali, wanted him to come visit him in the ancestral village, there was no way that he could escape. His mother had simply packed his things, bought all the rations he would need while his father had given him a long boring lecture about going back to one's roots and learning about traditions. His sister had sympathized with him but couldn't resist teasing him too, ragging him about cooking, sweeping, fetching water and other chores they were expected to do at grandfather's house; no complaints tolerated.

Sanen's grandfather lived alone, in the house he had built, and where he had lived with his wife and children for many happy years. He worked the rice fields that he had inherited from his father and rued that after he was gone, his two town-influenced sons and their uppity wives would surely neglect this work. Sanen's mother was the one who always dragged him and his father and sister every year to visit Awo Tali; Sanen thought that they were the only ones who had any links to grandfather, and so out of pity he had reluctantly agreed to spend his winter holidays with him.

However, after a few days of following his spry grandfather down steep hills to cut bamboo and carry it up to the village, he was having second thoughts. While Awo Tali would hardly speak except to point out the surrounding villages and the boundaries of the village land, Sanen would begrudgingly hack away at the bamboo, longing for the company of his own friends and the delights of Dimapur town.

But one cold January morning, Awo Tali took Sanen to a different area that he hadn't visited before. There was a bluish veil of pale mist swirling about the village giving it an eerie atmosphere. The single main road that meandered through the village divided it into the *ajen*, east, and *achep*, west. The houses on the eastern sides were more in number as the land sloped gently while on the western side the slope was steep. Most of the houses had matted bamboo walls and tin roofs, although there were a few concrete buildings that belonged to some big government officers who were from the village but lived in towns. Sanen and his grandfather walked briskly, leaving the village as people began to stir and signs of life were seen in some houses. Grandfather led him down a precarious footpath on the edge of a steep slope.

Oh man, where on earth is this old man taking me? Sanen wondered tiredly. He was half-asleep and still recovering from yesterday's chores. But he knew better than to say anything. The old man had his own ideas and Sanen knew he wouldn't get any answer even if he asked.

After what seemed like endless miles to Sanen, they reached the bottom of the slope and he noticed that the surrounding walls of the lower side of the slope had small cave-like holes dug out. Grandfather refreshed himself at the little stream nearby and pulled out from his old woven sling bag the *chachem*, food wrapped in leaves and tied with bamboo strings called *aling*. Silently he handed one to Sanen who had also refreshed himself and the two sat and ate the food, relishing every morsel. Sanen took out the water bottle from his knapsack and offered it to his grandfather who accepted it, took a small sip and handed it back. Sanen drank some water and feeling better, took stock of his surroundings. Oh man, we've walked down one hell of a steep hill, he thought. They had walked sixteen kilometres from the village, Awo Tali informed him as if reading his thoughts. Sanen groaned inwardly, now how the hell was he ever going to make it up? He took out the camera from his bag and started taking photos and was soon engrossed. Oblivious to his surroundings, Grandfather continued to sit there chewing contemplatively on his *khui*. Sanen went about clicking pictures and just as he was about done and wondering why his grandfather had brought him all the way down here, the old man stood up.

'Come on, young man, we have lots of work to do at home,' he said and picked up his sling bag and started walking. Sanen was exasperated. What did they come all the way down here for? But all he could do was follow suit and by late afternoon they were back in the village. Once they reached the house, they washed up and then set about making dinner. Once the dinner was made, the old man told Sanen to rest a bit, he was going out to feed his pigs and fetch water from the public tap on his way back. When Sanen awoke, it was already dark, grandfather had filled the big drum with water, swept the hearth and was sitting by the crackling fire whittling the bamboo to make *aling*. He smiled at Sanen and told him to serve out the dinner.

While they ate, grandfather casually mentioned that the place where they had gone today was the place called Lithu where Sanen's grandmother, Azao Temsu, used to go to collect the earth for making her earthen pots. The small cave-like holes at the bottom of the hill were the result of their digging because the earth inside had fewer stones and was better. The women from the village would trek to the site and dig out the earth and carry it back up the steep slopes in cane baskets, on their backs, with a head strap. Sanen looked at his grandfather and had to laugh to himself. Aha, a lesson taught, he thought.

On the day he had arrived, grandfather had asked how his mother was and Sanen had laughingly told his grandfather that his mother's manic obsession with the earthen pots was driving everyone at home crazy. His mother had inherited the pots from her mother and grandmother and had also collected some old ones over the years. About twenty pots of varying sizes lined the shelf above the mantlepiece while two pots were strategically placed near the fireplace, giving it a rustic set-up. She would constantly scold the maid to be careful when she swept the hearth, yell at Sanen and his sister Narola if they horsed around the kitchen throwing things at each other, and would be nagging her husband about making cabinets for her precious pots as the shelf was not very safe. Grandfather did not find it funny. He just gave Sanen a kindly smile.

Sanen looked at his grandfather again. He was sprightly and lean, not very tall, but strong. His shock of coarse white hair was cropped short. He was unlike any old man Sanen had ever met, he never lectured and spoke little. Sanen finished eating in silence. He understood. His grandfather did not mention the trek again.

The next day after helping his grandfather with the chores in and around the house, Sanen decided to visit his grandmother's cousin, Azao Senti, who lived in the upper *khel* of the village. She was also the master pot maker in the village. The old woman trilled and fussed over him. She was so happy to see her grand-nephew or grandson as she called him.

'And how is your grandfather, that old rascal? He must be deafening you with his constant chatter,' she laughed at her own joke. 'Do you know, the other day I asked him if he could lend me some money and he did not say a word, just brought me some earth and dumped it in the house and walked out.'

Sanen was puzzled. 'Why did he do that?'

'*Ayah*! You simpleton! He knew I needed the money to hire people to get the earth for me so he did just that. He brought the earth for me, and now there will be no question of repayment, or non-repayment!'

Breathlessly she went on talking about the hardships of getting good earth for making pots; her old bones were too worn out and she did not have the strength to carry the head-load anymore. Why, in her heyday she could carry twice the load that anyone could, and not only that, sometimes she trekked down to the Lithu three times a day. Ah, those were the days. She could make at least thirty to forty pots a day, and each time, the lot would be snapped up. She giggled, recalling the fights people used to have over her pots; they used to be in such high demand.

Sanen asked her how the pots were made and the old lady couldn't contain herself. 'Why do you want to know? Silly boy, you should know by now that men do not make pots. It's a woman's job,' she laughed at Sanen as she made tea and brought out the special biscuits which she kept hidden in a big earthen pot.

Sanen was quizzed about his mother, father and sister and everything about his life. He quickly finished the tea and left. Azao Senti could be shrill and her constant chatter and nosiness gave him a headache. All he had wanted to know was how the pots were made. Well, he would have to ask his grandfather.

That evening when Sanen asked his grandfather how the pots were made, his grandfather gave him a look of utter disbelief that said, 'That is women's work, how would I know?'

Just then, Sanen's phone rang. It was Narola, saying that she would be coming to the village the next day. Sanen was surprised. Why? The phone went dead. His grandfather smiled when he informed him Narola was coming. She was his pet.

Narola was twenty-one, petite, with very long hair which she was extremely proud of. The long hair made her look even more waif-like and fragile, but she was a headstrong girl, and most people said she was like her late maternal grandmother.

The next day around midday, Sanen and his grandfather waited at the bus stop at Aodang, the village square in the lower khel, as the old village bus chugged into view. Narola, looking distinctly dishevelled, got down from the bus shakily. Her grandfather gave her a formal handshake and, without a word, picked up her luggage and marched off towards his house in the Tsünglikiong area. Narola gave her brother a quick hug and they followed after the old man. Depositing her bags in the room they were to share, Sanen pounced on his sister, why was she in the village? She simply shrugged and told him that grandfather had sent word for her to come. Then she proceeded to ignore him, walking out of the room and bustling around the house, and chatting with her grandfather as she unpacked a basket and took out an assortment of stuff for him.

After dinner that evening, their grandfather's widowed sister, Azao Alemla, dropped in, agitated that the old man had not informed her of their visit.

'*Ayah*! This old man is such a clam, he uses his mouth only to eat fish and meat; to get words out of him is like extracting gold from the middle of the earth!' She poked her finger at the old man who only grunted and continued whittling the bamboo for his *aling*.

'Look at you Narola! Your hair suits you, never cut it off, let's see how long it is, goodness it touches your bum. You've got your granny's complexion, like the white roses your mother grows in her garden.' She looked at Narola admiringly. 'You are a beauty!'

Then she turned to him, 'Ah, Sanen, you are as lanky and grumpy like your grandfather here, poor you, you have the same coarse hair too, be warned you will have white hair before long!'

Then she addressed her brother, 'By the way, Tali, that over-smart lady who was after you has finally trapped a fool from the Merakiong locality. By God, you have been saved!' She cackled while grandfather gave her a dark look.

This was news. Narola started quizzing her grandfather, and soon both the women were mercilessly teasing the old man. The lady in question was a widow who had decided that their grandfather needed a woman and that she was the one. Over three years she had stalked him, chased him and tried every trick in the book to get him to marry her. Azao Alemla, helpless with laughter, gasped out that the widow had run out of steam and patience and had fixed her sights on another hapless gentleman who had succumbed to her wiles. The thought of anyone, let alone a lonely widow, trying to seduce their grandfather was too wild.

Grandfather suddenly got up and without a word walked out of the house, leaving the three of them helpless with laughter.

'Your grandfather is embarrassed!' Azao Alemla exclaimed gleefully. 'My dears, isn't this a nice surprise, the two of you all by yourself without your parents!'

Come to think of it, Sanen thought, that's true. All the years that they had visited the village, it was always as a family and since the visits were short, a week at the most, his parents would be busy dragging them around to meet all the relatives and friends.

'Don't mind your grandfather, he will always be like a stone, but he has a good heart, bless him. I'm sure he is bursting with happiness now that you are both here, you two were always his favourites, you know. I'm sure he simply ordered your mother to send you two to come and stay a few days with him!'

Turning to Sanen she went on, 'Now, I heard you two went down to Lithu yesterday. What was my brother thinking? It's so far, it's about sixteen kilometres from here, isn't it?'

Sanen recounted his conversation with his grandfather regarding his mother's obsession with the earthen pots. Azao Alemla laughed, 'Ah Sanen, you gave your grandfather a chance to visit Lithu and maybe bring back fond memories of your grandmother.'

'Well, he certainly didn't share any with me,' Sanen commented wryly.

This sent Azao Alemla into another spasm of laughter. 'That will be the day!' she howled.

'I have heard so many stories about their love story, please tell us the details!' Narola piped up.

Grandmother had died when they were very young and they hardly had any recollections of her except that she was always making pots whenever they visited.

Azao Alemla became quiet. Her eyes took on a faraway look. Pensively she remarked, 'Who would have thought my stony brother would have such a capacity to love a woman so completely? But then I guess the fire in your grandfather's heart burns deep and silent.'

'Well, when he was twenty-five, he decided that your grandmother was the one for him and he made it known to her through her cousin. Now your grandmother was five years older than him and she sent word through the same cousin, not to be over smart and to play with children his own age. She had a sharp tongue and men were afraid of her, besides, she was also more interested in making pots than in marrying. Her parents, of course, were only too happy. Their old maid finally had someone brave enough to want

49

to take her on and that too in marriage! They encouraged your grandfather and made a fuss over him whenever they met him. They even went so far as to tell our parents that the marriage should be fixed as soon as possible.'

Azao Alemla looked seriously at the youngsters listening attentively. 'Now that was a breach of traditions; the man's family makes the proposal and fixes the marriage date and so on. We all went against your grandfather's choice and this made him all the more determined, but he was also thwarted every step of the way by your grandmother, for almost three years. She would insult him, call him names, mock him and once when he visited her, she rubbed soot from the earthen pot on her face and acted like a mad woman. All this had no effect and I think in the end she agreed to marry him just so that the whole village would stop being entertained! It was the talk of the village and your grandfather's friends even put up a skit one Christmas-eve depicting their courtship in the variety show.'

Sanen and Narola could imagine just how hilarious that particular variety show must have been. They had witnessed a few over the years and had found the exaggerated stories and over-the-top costumes, makeup and humour quite gross, but it was greatly entertaining to the audience, especially as they knew the people who were being depicted in the skits.

'Anyway, they got married, much against our wishes,' Azao Alemla continued, 'and after they got married your grandmother continued making pots, while your grandfather worked hard on the rice fields. Your grandfather would do most of the household chores during the pot making season and let me tell you, it made my blood boil! That stupid, hen-pecked idiot, I used to think. Who told him to marry such a selfish woman? She was making my brother the laughing stock of the village. But, your grandmother was also very hard working, and since she was one of the master pot makers in the village, her pots sold out every time and that's how your uncles and mother could be sent out to be educated. Your grandmother insisted on that. They studied in Impur and in Mokokchung and that's how they went on to become big shots in the government service.'

Narola made tea and Azao Alemla, being alone and with nothing else to worry about settled down comfortably, visibly warming up to her story and enjoying being the centre of attention to two very curious youngsters.

'Your grandmother was a hellcat when it suited her, but over the years, she mellowed. Her family kept telling her that she did not deserve such a good man who loved her so unconditionally, and that must have seeped into her head because she began to be more appreciative of your grandfather and would often tell me how lucky she was. And I would tell her never to forget that.' Smiling at the memory, Azao Alemla sipped her tea slowly.

'Your grandfather used to follow your grandmother to Lithu to help her dig and carry the earth for her pots and he would be the butt of all the jokes because he was the only male around. The women were merciless in teasing him but I think secretly they envied your grandmother a lot! In our village the lot of women is hard, they have to cook, clean, look after husband, children, in-laws, pigs, chickens, the rice fields, the list goes on.'

'People would often make fun of your grandfather, but then he is made of stone, so whatever people called him or told him, it made no difference to him. He did what he thought was right, and what he enjoyed doing. But you know, everyone respects him because he is straightforward, honest and kind, and calls a spade a spade if the situation warrants.'

The three of them huddled around the fire sitting on the low wooden seats Awo Tali had made.

'When Azao Temsu died, did Awo Tali cry? Especially when he had to speak during her funeral?' Narola asked. She couldn't imagine her grandfather showing any public display of emotions. Narola and Sanen had not been taken to the village for the funeral as they had their final exams then and had been left behind in the charge of their father's cousin.

Azao Alemla sighed, 'You know, your grandmother died suddenly, she died in her sleep and it must have been a shock for your grandfather, and as usual, he was like a stone at first.

'But you know, once he started, your grandfather was quite poetic in his eulogy for his wife, the master pot-maker, who had lived life the way she saw fit. He said that his wife had supported the family by the sweat of her brow. The back-breaking toil, strength, and skills required for pot making is something only a woman knows, and she knew it too well. But, she had a deep abiding love for pottery, respect for the earth, and total commitment to her craft which she had learned from her mother and grandmother. She had taught many youngsters and her legacy now lives on through them. Her hands spoke for her and thus shaped the destiny of her family.'

Azao Alemla smiled, 'I tell you, I was so impressed and proud of your grandfather that day. For the final goodbye, all he said was, 'Now you are one with the earth you so loved, so don't look back, go, cross the river, and we will meet again one day.'

Sanen pensively stoked the fire. Awo Tali in all simplicity had shown him the legacy of his grandmother.

'Ah, I hope I find a man like grandfather,' Narola sighed.

Azao Alemla smiled and the three of them sat around the fire's warm glow, lost in thought.

Hekütha Qhumi
The Village Woman's Loom

ABOKALI JIMOMI

You wait for dawn spinning possibilities with patience
As the light bursts and its first rays flutter through leaves
your heart leaps, hurrying to harvest the sun's radiance
You set the threads in tension and hum as the loom weaves.

Your footrest firm, your head bent in concentration
your eyes moving in unison as the shuttle travels
like shooting stars at night darting across the blackness
carrying wefts of colour through the shed of emptiness.

The polished wood a sword your stable hands manoeuvre
To skilfully beat the yarn Thud! Thud! Thud! Creating
Patterns that outlast lifetimes like a fascinating fable of yore
Industry and love braided into your loom unwavering.

You imagine full and ripe colours of your paddy field
Dots of yellow you embroider a hundred tiny suns
Your soul in rhythm with red black green threads in motion
Your waist strapped by leather and determination

Scenes of hope you weave into the story of your Hekütha
Qhumi
Beaming as it comes alive piece by piece, your fatigue long
forgotten
You hope it will buy your children beautiful dreams

This Hekütha Qhumi
Dreamer, worker, woman

How precious your magic loom of wood and cotton!

Storyteller

EMISENLA JAMIR

It happened a long time ago, in another life, when I was young just like you. I see the little girl I was then, but she is not me and I am not her. No, you won't understand. It's frightening to think that I'll forget her, that everything I've seen and heard will be buried, lost. That's why I called you here. I've been watching you now for a while, and I can tell you love stories just as much as I love telling them. So, pay close attention and listen. I shall tell you a new story you've never heard before, of memories, mine, and those of people who have gone before me. And after I'm gone, when you sit by the fireplace warming your old bones during the harsh winters, you will remember how the fire crackled and warmed your young hands. You will remember today, and they will watch as the memories emerge out of your lips as your stories.

As I look back, I see the world through the eyes of the little girl. It looks young like I was then. Not young like the children these days. Things were simpler then. There were hardly any cars, and the phones and the computers that you cannot live without nowadays, they were undreamt of. But, things were easier then, gentler. Raids from the neighbouring villages had become a thing of the past. Life no longer revolved around head-hunting raids. There was a quiet rhythm in our lives. We did not want much. There were only a few offices to go to in those days, although things were certainly starting to change. So, we did what we usually did and worked in the fields.

A cousin of mine became a nurse though. When her mother could not persuade her daughter to stay at home and help with the household chores like all the other girls, she wept loudly. I can still see it clearly as if it happened yesterday. She stood by the doorway and wailed that her daughter was going to become a *tsumar*. How I wanted to laugh! As if going to a new place would transform her features into that of a plainsfolk. How simple I was then! Only a few years later did I realize what my aunt had actually meant. My cousin returned a qualified nurse, but there was something different about her. Her skin had not changed as I had imagined, but she was different in a way that I couldn't quite grasp. I did feel a twinge of envy every now and then when mother talked of her knowledge of medicines and her service to the village folk. But I didn't think much of it. You see, I had no big dreams of becoming a nurse. All I ever wanted to be was a storyteller.

You may laugh at my youthful dreams now, but it was a true yearning. I wanted to be like Otsüla. I would watch her closely and listen keenly as the words effortlessly rolled off her lips. There never was an old story. Every re-telling brought a new dimension to the stories and we never got bored of listening to them. Or even if the rest of the children found them boring, I never did. We would all sit around the fire-place in the middle of the kitchen and listen to her. Her stories were endless. She told us tales of Rangtsüngba and how he killed Salunaro. She told us of the legendary lovers Jina and Etiben and we laughed when Etiben blackened her face to repel the advances of an unwanted suitor. I lived every one of those lives. I was there when Longkongla went up the rope to flee from the enraged villagers. But she just couldn't help herself. She had to look down, didn't she? People these days don't want to remember. They don't want to look back lest they fall like Longkongla. They think it is better to move forward into the new world, the future. But what will happen to them when they want to come back? And what if there is no home for them to come back to? Who will tell them of their past?

But, I digress. Please forgive the wandering mind of an old woman! I have much to tell, but there is so little time. Where was I? Ah, the storyteller! I admired her tremendously. No, no, she was no great beauty. But the way she wove the words was truly beautiful. And I kept saying to myself, if only I had such mastery with words, I could care less for beauty. She held us enthralled with her stories and many a time when the parents came to pick up their children, they too would sit down quietly and listen to her, forgetting the reason for their coming. I imagine even time stopped to listen to her stories. They were so clear then, the stories. Now, they are all vague and neglected. People don't realize the worth of such stories.

One day, my mother had sent me to Otsüla's house with some *angu pongsen*. She lived some five houses away from ours and my mother would often send her food. Her husband had died years ago and now she lived alone. Her children lived close by though, so she always had company. She must have been about my age now, old and wrinkly, like me. Funny! Perhaps one day, when you grow old with wrinkles on your hands and face you'll remember me. Aah, now, now, don't look so alarmed. You still have time on your side, at least for a while.

So, carrying the fish I went to her house. I looked around and found her sitting alone on the *machang*, staring dreamily into space. My footsteps roused her from her reverie and she turned and smiled at me. 'What is this? Is that fish I smell?' she said. 'Oja cooked it,' I told her and shyly handed her the bowl. Yes, it's hard to think that I was a shy person. Much has changed since then. She told me she loved fish and started telling me a story of one of her father's fishing trips. He and his friend had put in their fishing lines for quite a long while now but there were still no signs of any fish in the water. Then in the quiet of the jungle, they heard a group of men fishing a little way downstream. So he and his friend decided to head there and join them. They followed the sounds of fishing but each time they thought they had reached the place, it sounded like it was just a bit farther downstream from where they stood. This kept on happening and then suddenly just as they were getting really exasperated, her father saw wet footprints on the rocks. He saw that the footprints led towards the sound. Water was still trickling down from the footprints, and he knew immediately that someone must have just walked past them. But it confused him at first. It was as if the owner of the print was walking backwards. Then her father felt a chill go down his spine. He silently motioned to his friend pointing to the fresh footprints on the large river rocks. They knew then that it was futile to fish that day. They had encountered Aonglemla, the guardian of the forest. How cleverly she had tricked them from fishing! Some people dismiss stories like these as superstition. But how can it be superstition when it actually happened? As Otsüla was telling me the story, the hair on my arms stood up and I felt afraid to go back home alone. But I ran as fast as I could and managed to reach home without any unearthly encounters. After that, whenever I finished my chores, I would rush over to Otsüla's house and sit there, listening to the tales of old.

I never forgot that Aonglemla story, though. Somehow, the lonely creature that dissuaded the men from fishing that day stuck to me. She was supposed to be a terror. Anyone who was unfortunate enough to chance upon her supposedly died soon after. Was it a curse that led her to live such a lonely life? People often heard her laughing in the jungles. Most would run off leaving their baskets half filled with firewood and return only when they felt it was safe enough to get their things back. I was in the woods one day, gathering firewood with my friends when I heard someone laughing. It was more of a cackle, really. My friends began to gather their baskets, whispering furiously that it was Aonglemla. I wanted to see this creature that everyone was terrified of, but my friends told me to stop being an idiot and dragged me along with them.

I'd like to think that the old trees were sharing some ancient stories with Aonglemla and that she must have been laughing at something funny that a young tree innocently remarked upon. Her voice, unused for centuries, must have startled us, frightening my friends into abandoning the forest. I regret not staying around longer. I often imagine her listening to the complaints of the fish as she looked at herself in the rippling water. Did she move her hair to reveal her face to herself? Did her feet ache as she moved away from the people and into the arms of the forest she'd made her home? I wanted to see her, to listen to her story, but I only heard of her. Never from her. Maybe you will have better luck than I did.

But I was telling you about Otsüla. Where were we? Yes. So, not long after I visited Otsüla, I was sweeping the house one day, when a young boy came over and told me that she wanted to see me in the afternoon. I wondered what it was about because she had never sent for me before. The whole day I was uneasy. I finished my duties and asked my mother if I could go and see her. Since mother was there when the boy brought the news, she agreed. Otsüla was sitting on the machang smoking her pipe. When she saw me she stood up and went inside the house. I followed her into the kitchen but she went straight to her room. I did not know if I was supposed to follow her, so I waited until I heard her call my name. Gingerly I stepped into her room. She was sitting on her bed. She looked so frail, but her eyes were bright and alert. 'You must be wondering why I called you,' she said smiling. I merely nodded. 'Remember you once asked how I became a storyteller?' I nodded again. 'I listened,' she said simply. 'Like you. I listened to all the stories of old and kept them in my head and in my heart. Everything was in the stories, you just had to look. I became one with each of the stories and they have been ever faithful to me. Stories stay in your head and they also connect with your heart.'

Then Otsüla took my hands in hers and raised my left hand up to her head and my right to her heart. 'I am old now, and I don't know if I'm going to find *Meyutsüngba* or *Yisu* when I die, but I want to leave behind the stories with

61

someone who knows their value. As she said this, she slowly touched her forehead. 'Come, child what do you see?' she asked. I was a little frightened but my curiosity got the better of me. I looked, but all I could see was aging skin and grey hair. I didn't want to be rude so I told her I saw nothing. 'Look closely child, what do you see?' she asked again. This time I saw a thin reddish line run from her hairline to the back of her head and I became alarmed. 'What is that? Does it hurt? Should I call mother?' I asked. 'Don't be silly', she replied, 'Just help me get this off.' But I didn't know what she was trying to remove. I was just beginning to think that maybe old age had finally addled her senses when I saw the line on her head move. Immediately I knew exactly what Otsüla wanted me to help her with.

I held the sides of her head firmly, just above the ears, and pulled in an upward motion. The whole thing came off cleanly, like a lid, but I dared not look inside. I had seen the insides of slaughtered animals enough to know that I did not want to look inside. Otsüla calmly put her hands inside her head and took out an object. It wasn't covered in blood as I had feared. On the contrary, it was black, like it had been kept near the fireplace for a long time to get smoked. It was one of the finest pots I had ever seen, small and perfectly proportioned. It held all my attention and I momentarily forgot all about the unbelievable scene that I had just been a part of.

By the time I looked up, Otsüla looked perfectly normal and there was no line on her forehead. 'This is for you,' she said to me. 'It holds treasures far greater than any wealth, and I want you to have it before I die. My children, they love me, but they don't care so much for the stories. They listen just to indulge me. But you, you know better. You know how irreplaceable they are. So I'm handing you what the storyteller of my time once handed over to me.' With this, she placed the pot inside my head. I felt nothing really, and when I woke up the next day, I thought it had just been a dream. And when I went to visit Otsüla, it was as though she had been waiting for me, and as always I sat and listened to her tell the stories of long ago. She died a few weeks after that and I grieved deeply for this great loss.

I did not immediately become a storyteller. The pot of stories took time to brew. But slowly and steadily I found my voice. I told you, I used to be a shy girl. But when I told stories, I became a different person. I became more alive through the telling of my stories. That's what my friends used to say. And so, I've been telling my stories ever since. Now, you must be wondering why I called you today. Ah, clever! You know! Yes, child, I believe it's time.

Untitled

KUTOLI N

Watercolour on paper.

Cherry Blossoms in April

EASTERINE KIRE

April 1944, Rusoma Village, Nagaland.

The Japanese soldiers came marching into the village in a long column, raising dust from the hard ground with their black boots, and much to the people's surprise, the first man addressed them in English and Hindi, before translating his leader's words:

'If you give us food and shelter, no harm will come to you. We are your friends. We have come to liberate you from the British. Do not fear us. We will not harm you.'

The Japanese chose to stay at the Gaonbura's house because it was not only spacious but also provided a good view of the approach road to the village. Keeping calm, the elders of the village accommodated them, and yet the distrust of these men, who looked so much like them but spoke an altogether strange language, never quite left their hearts.

The advance of the Japanese into Naga villages in the east had been so sudden that the countryside was overrun by them in no time. Fear of these invading troops had preceded their coming for a long time. A sense of unease had spread over all the northern Angami villages until whole populations evacuated their homes and began camping in their fields. The populace of Kohima village had also fled and was now using the small field-huts as shelters. With the Japanese occupying their village, they scavenged for food in the forests and, only by night, carried back grain from their granaries.

This was the fate of most villages in the path of the Japanese invasion. Prior to their arrival, the Angami people had conveyed the news from village to village, 'The Japanese are coming! The Japanese are coming!' Many rumours had sailed back and forth between villages before their actual arrival. 'They are fierce and heartless!' was often repeated, and stray stories of what they had done to the Chinese population added to the people's deep dread of them.

But Rusoma people did not leave their village. They had felt fairly secure about staying on because the Japanese occupiers were not unfriendly. They had been asked to provide rations, which they gave in the Naga spirit of hospitality. No sojourner who asked for food was refused. That he might become a foe later was never reason to refuse him food. So they came to stay, the short stocky soldiers who guarded the Gaonbura's house, and their officers who were taller and better dressed. The village elders had waited to receive them in the village with sinking hearts.

Sanuo was one of the young women who, along with her aunt, had watched the entry of the Japanese into their village. She looked on curiously as the elders spoke to the Japanese and made arrangements to host them. Some of the foreign men looked lean and hungry. Their leader was smart and short-haired. He smiled in a strange manner. The smile never reached his eyes. She watched him converse with the Gaonbura. He smiled as he tried to make his points clear and yet he looked every inch capable of eliminating anybody who stood in his way. The hardness of the man was only just held back by the veneer of friendliness. The officer suddenly turned in Sanuo's direction and she quickly averted her eyes. But he had seen her quick movement and laughed out loud in the knowledge of it. She hurriedly moved away from the courtyard and tried to mingle with the other women so that he would not know it was she who had been watching him so intently. Those hard, hard eyes. They were so frightening.

The officers settled into their camp, the Gaonbura's house, and as the weeks went by, more and more soldiers arrived in the village. With every increase in numbers of soldiers, the villagers grew alarmed that the Japanese presence would draw British fire. However, the Japanese and their Indian scouts assured them they would not stay long. In the meantime though, they needed the village to help them out with food and shelter for which they would be compensated within a few weeks time. That was what they said.

Although the villagers expressed their reservations about continuing to host the Japanese, the truth was they did not have much choice in the matter. To refuse them entry would have resulted in the deaths of the Gaonbura and other village elders. They had heard of men in Kohima village shot dead by the Japanese for refusing to carry ammunition loads for them.

'Stay out of their way!' warned the elders, 'Soldiers are not ordinary men. They who have tasted war have been known to do terrible things. Women, cover yourselves modestly so no harm will come upon you, for we are not able to protect you.'

The women knew only too well what was meant. Women had been raped by the Japanese in some of the villages. Those accounts were spoken about in hushed whispers. These were too terrible thoughts to dwell upon and women shushed each other, 'Oh, may it never be any one of us.'

The men were forced to work for the Japanese. There was no way they could avoid it. Groups of men laboured each day, carrying ammunition across to the next village. They used the smaller pathways because the main one was frequently targeted by British bomber planes. Using the narrow forest trails was more difficult with the heavy loads they carried, but it was less risky. The younger men fetched water for the Japanese. The women pounded grain daily for them. But they kept a safe distance from the soldiers, who watched them lazily.

One morning, they heard a loud cry, 'More soldiers are coming!' Half an hour later, they saw uniformed figures walking along the path just outside the village gates. A small force of the Japanese was on their way to the village. An officer was in the lead. When they came through the village gate, the children were the first to greet them. An urchin marched up to them with a stick which he used as a gun and saluted them smartly. The grimness of the first encounter was suddenly dispelled and the soldiers smiled at the urchin's action. The tension dissolved and the men were led away by the children to the Gaonbura's house. Just then, one of the watching villagers said loudly,

'Look at their leader, he is different, he is so fine!'

The young officer looked as weary as his soldiers but he was a handsome man, and all the villagers looked at him with new eyes, wondering how one so fair could choose the life of a soldier, filled with so much violence. The young man felt their gaze on him and he turned around and smiled weakly.

'Ah, he is a fine one,' agreed another old woman loudly.

News travelled swiftly among the women. Despite the situation, their interest was aroused and they all endeavoured to get a look at this new officer. They were not disappointed. He was tall and fair. Very different from his superior, the cold-eyed officer. When the young officer saw the children, he smiled at them and offered Japanese money which the children scrambled to get. How did he come to be here? Was he a rich man's son? Did he have sisters and brothers at home? A wife? Never had a Japanese soldier aroused so much curiosity among the villagers. The men did not think it frivolous of the women to talk so much of the young officer.

'He looks very refined indeed,' they all agreed, 'Not at all the sort to go to battle.'

Sanuo heard all this and was just as eager as all the other women to see the young man. It was her turn the next day to pound grain and carry it to the Gaonbura's house where the senior Japanese officer and his bodyguards were lodged. In the beginning, the men had carried the grain, but when weeks passed without incident they had relaxed their guard and let their women take it. Sanuo finished pounding the grain and walked over to the large house with her grain-basket on her back. In the courtyard, she lifted her basket strap off her forehead and rested it on her shoulders. Her load felt heavier, but in this way she could look around to see those living in the house. A movement to her left startled her. She turned to look. It was a Japanese soldier cleaning his gun. Alarmed, she quickly lifted the basket strap to her head, walked into the granary, emptied the basket and hurried home with her heart pounding. The fear of guns had driven off all thoughts of seeing the handsome young man who had caught the imagination of the whole village.

Three days later, Sanuo was at the stream with a group of women who had gone there to bathe and wash clothes. Sometimes the Japanese soldiers would walk out of the woods and walk past the women in the stream. The women chattered among themselves as they washed and bathed. It was surprising how the reality of the war could sometimes be forgotten when doing these activities together. It was almost like the old days.

One of them spoke aloud, 'Perhaps our Sanuo should marry the young Japanese. He is so handsome he should leave some seed behind.'

Sanuo blushed at their words. She was not used to the way they teased her; when she blushed at their coarse joking, they teased her even more mercilessly. This kind of banter was common among most of the women. If she wanted their company she would have to put up with them and joke along and try to divert their attention elsewhere. As the women were laughing and chattering, two figures came up to the edge of the water. The women stopped laughing when they saw that the object of their attention was standing right there at the water's edge watching them.

An elder woman stood up and boldly said, 'We were teasing your wife a little.'

The young officer could not understand her words but he waved at them finding nothing threatening about a group of women bathing. He smiled at the women without seeming to focus on any one face. Then he turned and led the other soldier away with him.

When they were gone, Sanuo said, 'He is really very good looking.'

The others laughed and the woman who had addressed the Japanese captain said, 'That's why we are saying you should marry.'

Later that night, Sanuo's head was full of thoughts. She lay in bed, listening to the sounds from the village and the gunfire from the direction of Kohima. These sounds that were so new to them, but which in the past weeks they had come to live with. When morning came, Sanuo had overslept and so she rushed to the water spot to fetch water. She finished filling her pot and stood up to twist her hair into a bun. As she was about to lift her water-pot it was suddenly taken from her hands and before she could react, the same hands carefully placed it in her carrying basket. Stifling her instinct to cry out, she turned around and found the young officer smiling down at her. So it was he and not one of her friends who had put the water-pot into her basket. How she blushed. Oh, where were the words to thank him? Still, she managed to mumble out some thanks in her own tongue. He smiled at her and stood watching as she walked away. No one had witnessed the incident.

Later, when Sanuo stood pouring the water into the large container at home, she could not stop trembling. His nearness had made her feel strange. The sudden sight of his face above hers had made her heart beat violently and she wondered why he made her feel that way. So different from any of the boys in her age group. When the Japanese first came, everyone had been saying harsh things about them. The women had hidden from them for a long time. But in all the weeks that they had been there, no one in the village had been harmed by them. The young village boys had been the first to make friends with the soldiers, following them into the woods and playing with them when they were relaxing in their camps. But there had always been a certain reserve between the women and the Japanese soldiers. She dare not think further. But, wasn't he so much like the sky-husbands Grandmother used to tell her about? The delicately beautiful men who came down from the skies to seek wives among earth-women? He had the same line of cheek and chin that she had imagined when she listened to Grandmother describe them. It was now two years since she had died, and now no one would ever tell those stories again.

Sanuo had had a dream once, while her grandmother was still alive. Her room had filled up with a very bright light and a beautiful man, her sky-husband, had stood there, holding out his hands toward her. Her grandmother had died exactly a month after that strange dream and she had always wondered: had he not come for her and instead taken Grandmother by mistake?

A newcomer to the village would think Sanuo rather plain looking at first sight, but she too had her own share of delicacy. On closer observation, one would see the fine bones defining a face that made her stand out from the other girls who were pretty only in an earthy way. Sanuo was light-limbed, not likely to turn stodgy in middle age. And right now, with her face flushed from her encounter with the Japanese officer, she looked radiant. It must have been this that he had seen in her.

Nobody knew Sanuo's birth date but her grandmother had said she was born the year they built the new church. That was eighteen and a half years ago. With her grandmother now gone, Sanuo lived all by herself in the small house they had shared. Both her parents had died of an epidemic of malaria when she was barely four years old. That she was living on her own was a little unusual in a village where orphaned children were brought up by grandparents or relatives. Her maternal uncle had invited her to come and live with them but Sanuo knew her uncle's wife was a mean woman and would likely mistreat her. So she stayed on in her grandmother's house with the excuse that she felt sorry to abandon it.

The next day, the whole village was summoned to a meeting. One of the elders interpreted for the senior Japanese officer who stood at the head of the gathering and spoke in English. His speech went along the usual lines: No one was to report any of their activities to the British forces. If they caught anyone doing that, they would be forced to kill that person. Because this was war. But they must understand that the Japanese army did not regard the Nagas as their enemies. They were of the same race and therefore it was only right that they should help one another. This was the sort of speech that the villagers were now used to hearing once a week or so.

Sanuo stood at the back of the gathering and looked in the direction of the young officer whilst his superior was giving his speech. She saw his eyes searching the crowd overtly, appearing as though it was routine for him to do so. When he saw her he smiled ever so slightly and she blushed and looked down. It was amazing how he disturbed her feelings so.

As soon as the meeting was over the crowd dispersed. Sanuo slipped away trying to avoid coming face to face with him. When she was at a safe distance she looked back. He had been watching her all the while and when she stopped to look he made as though he would come after her, but she retreated swiftly and he turned away as well.

When night fell, she lay in bed, sleepless. What were those feelings that had come over her at the sight of the stranger? She had not even exchanged two words with him. Why did she feel so strongly drawn to him? Could this be love? That's crazy, she thought. Then, she heard soft footfalls at her doorstep. Probably her uncle to see she was all right. He did that sometimes. There was a knock on the door. She slipped out of bed and went to unlatch it. The young officer stood there smiling at her. Then he moved quickly into the house so that she had to move back in order not to be squashed up against him. The next moment, her hands were in his and he was saying soft things to her in Japanese. He touched her hair and forehead every now and then, holding her hands tenderly. There was no resistance in her now and she leaned into him feeling safe, right, and fulfilled. Her sky-husband had come to her at last.

In the morning, she went to the Gaonbura's house and when that venerable gentleman appeared she told him without mincing her words, 'We are man and wife now, the young one and I. I am not his concubine but he is my husband. For as long as destiny will allow us.'

The old man saw the happiness in her eyes and the fulfillment that made her face glow and he said, 'It is well, my daughter, it is as it should be. Go and care for your husband.'

Then he went and spoke to the two officers, the hard one and the young one. He first addressed the young officer, 'She is given to you to be your wife, not your concubine. Look after her well, she is a good woman.' Then, turning to the older Japanese he said, 'Let them be together. They are husband and wife now.' The senior officer assented. That same day, the young man moved into Sanuo's house and they lived as man and wife.

They were so happy together, laughing softly over their inability to communicate in words. When they lay together he expressed his love by stroking her hair gently for a long time. When he spoke to her in Japanese or in English, she smiled back and spoke a few words of love in her language. And he, her sky-husband, could not understand a word she said to him, only that they sounded beautiful, and he knew that she was loving him wordlessly and with words which while making no sense to him conveyed all of her feelings. Kuniyuki, that was his name, and she would say it sweetly, calling him in when she had finished cooking their meal.

How many moments and hours and days did they have together? Absorbed in each other, transcending speech, using only their hands to tell each other their secrets and make each other happy. These are never the memories that remain and comfort. They are too fragile. Perhaps we were never meant to love on earth. The finest of love stories always end in death, or in parting. Perhaps we overreach ourselves when we love.

A month and a half of happiness. Just barely that long. The war, the war they had suspended with their loving, engulfed them again. Using a few words and a paper on which he drew pictures to show his fate to her, he made her understand that he had to go northward where the fighting was so fierce that no soldier could be spared. She had no questions for him because she had always known this was how their story would end. On the last night neither slept. They lay holding each other silently. When morning came, the harsh calls of an army on the move separated them.

They say he died in the war. When they found his body, there was among his papers a drawing of a cherry tree in full bloom and a woman seated below it, a woman with dark eyes and long black hair that fell to her waist.

First published in *Forest Song* (Barkweaver Publications, 2011).

The Letter

TEMSULA AO

There was an uneasy quiet in the village: the underground extortionists had come and gone and along with them the hard-earned cash the villagers had earned by digging the first alignment for a motorable road to their village. It was work that had been assigned to them by the Border Roads Organization after much lobbying and often acrimonious negotiations. The BRO had at first refused to outsource work to the villagers saying that they had enough manpower to dig the alignment by themselves. The villagers had countered by saying that since the road was being constructed through their land, as landowners they had to be involved in demarcating the route which, otherwise, might encroach on the territory of the neighbouring village, and which in turn might lead to unnecessary complications.

The contract was eventually awarded to them and they completed the work two days ahead of time. All those engaged in the work had different plans for spending the cash. A few of them wanted to put tin roofs on their houses; some had already entered into negotiations to buy pairs of bulls to plough their fields. One man had actually taken some planks from a neighbour on credit to repair his floor and was going to pay him off after he received his wages from the BRO.

What the villagers did not reckon with was the efficiency of the underground intelligence network.

On the very day that they were paid, some strangers entered their village at dusk. They ordered the frightened villagers to take them to the headman's house where they stated their demand. They read out the names of the villagers involved in the work and found one man was missing from the group. He was the same man who had bought the timber and was busy cutting it to size to repair the rotten floorboards. He was hauled in before the visitors who berated him soundly for ignoring their summons. The villagers sensed immediately that their plans for utilizing the hard-earned cash would come to naught because they knew that these fierce-looking goons from the forest had come to the village at night with only one purpose: to rob them in the name of the underground government. Resisting them was of no use: they carried guns and the consequences of any conflict would only mean retaliation.

Such acts of blatant extortion from the so-called 'national workers' was not a new thing for the simple villagers. What amazed them was the timing of their arrival and the accuracy of their information. They even had records of how much each labourer had received from the BRO! Now, in the presence of the headman, they began to read out how much each man had to pay them as 'tax'. With hatred in their hearts and murder in their eyes, the men started to count the amounts due from each and placed them in front of the headman. But one man was counting his money again and again. When he had done it several times he began to appeal to the leader, saying that he had to pay off his debt to the timber trader and if he gave them his due, he would not be able to send any money to his son who was to appear in the final examination of the year and needed to pay the examination fee within the week. He promised to pay them soon but requested that he be excused from the present reckoning; otherwise, his son would not be able to sit for the examination. This man had worked for fewer days because of his wife's illness and hence was paid the least amount. He even tried to explain this to the leader. But before he could complete the appeal, one of the extortionists shot out from the stool he was sitting on and hit the poor man with the butt of his rifle, 'What examination, what fees? Don't you know what sacrifices we have made in our fight against the government? And how we are suffering in the forest? Are you saying that we should not collect taxes so that your sons can give examinations and become big babus in the Indian government to rule over us?'

Even as he uttered the word 'Indian' his face seemed to distort with naked rage, like a fierce animal at the sight of an adversary. With the quickness born out of living in hostile surroundings, the headman pulled the fallen man aside, otherwise murder would have taken place at that very next moment. He also took the money from the injured villager and gave it to the still-angry man, asking him to leave immediately. Though the leader acted like he was offended by the tone of the headman, he complied because on many occasions he had been saved from the army patrolling parties by this man's advance warnings about their movements.

After the departure of the unwanted guests, the men began to administer first aid to the injured man. His face was already swelling, and his mouth and nose were bleeding. After cleaning him up as best as they could, they carried him to the village compounder who gave him some pills to stop the bleeding and told him to rest for a few days. In the meantime, the headman, realizing the plight of this unfortunate man, lent him some money which was sent to his son studying in a nearby town, to take care of his examination needs. Though the immediate danger was avoided, the villagers were apprehensive about the presence of underground elements in the vicinity. Lately, news had filtered in about the rogue elements in the movement who had taken to harassing simple villagers and townsfolk alike by collecting 'taxes' in the name of the underground government and using the money to feed their drug and drinking habits. There were even stories of how such characters were 'punished' by their superiors: with their hands and feet tied, they were shot in the head at point-blank range. What happened to these renegades was of little consequence to the villagers who knew they had to contend with not only these different types of underground elements but also with government agents and the Indian army.

The people in this village were generally known to be docile, trying their best to avoid conflict with both the overground and the underground governments. They were also on fairly good terms with the army personnel who came to their village occasionally to buy vegetables, rice, and other farm produce. But this incident seemed to have revived a dormant rage in their minds. In groups of twos and threes they began to discuss their grievances over a number of days. At home, in fields, and in forests their minds were filled with resentment and anger at the injustice inflicted on them over the years by the various players in Nagaland's murky politics;

together, they had plunged Naga society into anarchy. As though driven by a hidden force, they converged on the headman's house one evening and began a heated discussion. The elderly were more cautious and urged restraint. But the younger ones spoke for action against these forces and asked for retaliation against whoever henceforth treated them with disrespect and tried to 'steal' from them. The debate continued until the wee hours and the voice of the elders was drowned in the strong current of anger and resentment of the young. The village council finally resolved that they would cease to pay any 'tax' to the underground, would refuse to do 'free' labour for the government, and would discourage the army visits by refusing to sell any of their produce to them. This decision seemed to appease the anger of the youth and, with the first cock's crow, the elders cautioned the youth not to initiate any unprovoked hostility.

In spite of the resumption of apparent normalcy in the village, the story of the assault on the hapless man evoked strong reactions also from the women. In private they called their menfolk 'women' and taunted them by indirect remarks and bawdy songs about their emasculation. The men could do nothing about this because in their hearts they acknowledged the fact that they had indeed been cowed down for a very long time. But these emotional upheavals were soon overshadowed by everyday realities and the village once again returned to its placid ordinariness.

The calm, however, was not to last very long because when they least expected it, the inevitable happened.

It presented itself in the form of an armed man in the village asking for directions to the headman's house. The old woman who was thus accosted stood rooted to the spot.

She had just come out of her son's house where she had gone to give a special dish that she had cooked for her ailing grandchild. Though old and seemingly out of touch with the current events of the village, she had lived in 'grouping zones' during the peak of insurgency and survived beatings at the hands of the army. She had also seen the tortured victims, the so-called 'sympathizers' of the underground forces, and lived through the trauma in the wake of her husband's abduction and eventual killing by the underground on charges of being an informer and 'guide' of the Indian army. But this moment was epiphanic because, in spite of the camouflage uniform and the scraggly beard, she recognized the man as one of the abductors of her husband. Squinting her eyes to pretend nearsightedness and keeping her voice as calm as possible she gave him directions, not to the house of the headman but to that of one of the members of the younger group.

After he left, she retraced her steps to her son's house to inform him of what she had done. He, in turn, grabbed his shawl and dao and sprinted to his friend's house in order to collect the group. Then a group of seven men was seen marching towards the house where the stranger was confronting the owner, brandishing his gun and threatening him that if he did not collect a certain amount of money as 'emergency tax' imposed by the underground army he would kill him and his family and anyone who opposed him. Even as he finished saying this, he became aware of the group of villagers who surrounded him. Though he had his gun, he became terribly worried. Trying to put up a brave front, he challenged the newcomers, 'Who are you and why have you come here like this?'

At this, one of the group who was simply called Long Legs because of his height, countered his question, 'We should be asking *you* that,' and so saying tried to advance towards him. The stranger, by now thoroughly frightened by the menace surrounding him, fired his gun. But luckily the bullet only whizzed past one of the villagers and no one was injured. The sound of gunfire in the meantime brought many other villagers out of their homes, at first very cautiously, but when word spread that there was only one underground man they all made for the house in front of which the fracas was in progress. Seeing so many able-bodied men surrounding him, the man tried to run away but his way was blocked by the human wall. No one knew for sure who started the beating but it continued mercilessly for several minutes until the man lost consciousness and slumped to the ground in a bloody heap. Realizing the gravity of the situation, the rest of the villagers deserted the scene leaving the young activists with the injured man, inert and bleeding profusely.

The owner of the house was by now almost incoherent with fear about the consequences of this incident and begged the group to take the body as far away from his house as possible. Long Legs, the obvious leader of the group, instructed the others to lift the man. Telling them to follow him, he took them away from the village into a jungle path leading towards a ravine which was believed to be haunted by the ghost of a man who had fallen from a tree and dashed to his death on the stones below. It would soon be dark and the others protested that it was unsafe for them to venture into the unholy area. But he kept going, using his dao to clear the shrubbery on the trail. After much disgruntled huffing and puffing, the men reached a high point of the hillock with their burden.

Dumping the still-breathing man unceremoniously, the men sprawled on a clearing to rest awhile. They first made a bonfire in the middle with the dry wood and twigs lying nearby. It was obvious to every man what should happen to the inert body, but the question uppermost in everybody's mind was: how would it be done and what should they do afterwards? Long Legs himself seemed to be pondering the question: he was pacing around the body, his eyes riveted to the ground. Sensing that any delay would only cause more difficulties for them, he called the others together and asked them one question: should they leave the man to die where he was or should they hurl him off the cliff? The answer was unanimous: throw him off the cliff. Then what about his gun? That too, they replied. As the men were going to execute their decision, Long Legs cried out, 'Stop, let us at least find out who he actually was.' Once again, the men let go of the body; Long Legs started rummaging through the pockets of the stranger and pulled out a few sodden notes of small denominations, a tattered ID with almost illegible writing and a letter addressed to a post box of a nearby town. Having emptied the pockets, once again the men lifted the bloody heap which was once a man and to a collective count of three, hurled it to its final resting place. His gun too was tossed after him. This done, the men sat down once again as Long Legs examined each scrap of paper. He counted the notes and found that the man had exactly forty-nine rupees. The ID was unreadable, so was another piece of paper which also seemed to have been a letter once. Then he began reading the letter with the postbox number. As he continued reading, his face began to change and he slumped to the ground as if struck by something heavy. His mates, however, physically tired and drained of emotions, failed to observe the sudden change in Long Legs' demeanour. The gathering dusk also helped. The entire group seemed to be in some kind of stupor.

Long Legs was the first to recover; he picked up all the contents from the dead man's pocket and threw them into the dying fire. As the group watched the paper-pile disappear in the smoke, each of them felt as if a huge burden had been lifted from his shoulders. After taking an oath that they would never reveal what had happened to the stranger, they began walking towards the village in the gathering darkness with the help of torches made of bamboo and reeds.

The letter was Long Leg's personal cross as long as he lived. Though he had never been a good student he remembered every word of it, the letter from the dead man's son, begging the father to send his exam fees.

First published in *Laburnum For My Head* (Penguin, 2009), p. 54-62.

Sad Poems
(April 2018)

NAROLA CHANGKIJA

'I like sad poems,' she says,
'they curl inside you
like unborn babies, no?'
I don't know. Never had one.
Babies, I mean.
Poems, a few, many, I think.

All the good, the bad, the ugly
startled into life, randomly –
that zoo elephant joyous in her waterhole;
a friend's evil cockatoo locked in its cage;
the mango tree that gives and gives all summer long;
the old man and his dog,
sun-lit ghosts in the phantom cane fields,
where the new skyscrapers go babeling up,
ever up and away;

– such things can strike a verse, shape a poem,
seed and take root, maybe.

Then my mother takes another drag,
blows and sighs.
'We liked sad poems, your Abao and I.
Made us happy, made us twist, made us cry.
Write me a new one for old time's sake,
please, before I die of this ache.'

I take the cigarette from her.
I promise to write something new.
But I lied, of course,
as I flicked the ash
and stubbed the end
in the small space between their graves.

A Happening

EM EM EL

he was kind.
he was generous with his words.
he was honest.
he was true.
he was cold.
he didn't believe in Him.
his reasons were so valid.
she didn't want to change him.
she didn't want to hurt him.
she just wanted to live fearlessly.
love unwithholdingly.
speak truth boldly.
and in doing so, she wanted Love to be the reason he came
around.
that he comes back.

...

he came back.

Untitled

SIRAWON TULISEN KHATING

Mixed media: pencil/digital.

Konyak-Naga Folk Song

(sung by girls while they pound rice on the pounding table)

Translated by
PHEJIN KONYAK

I wish to remain at my parents' house forever,
I wish to be their little girl always,
I do not wish to become someone else's,
But my breasts and hips lie to me and they blossom
And like the ways of the world I will have to follow in the
footsteps of my mother and sisters
before me and marry someday and belong to someone else.

Collected from Shiyong village, Mon district, Nagaland. First published in
The *Konyaks: Last of the Tattooed Headhunters* (Roli Books, 2017), p. 31.

When I Was a Girl
(April 2018)

NAROLA CHANGKIJA

When I was a girl,
the world was mystery and locked doors,
the keys hung out of reach,
and in the quiet bedroom,
the soft shadow of Abao curled around Alao.

When I was a girl,
one winter's night in Phek town,
we heard a knock on the door;
but when we answered,
nobody stood there, only the leafless tree.

When I was a girl,
that summer night in Chumukedima,
I walked through a field of summer corn,
hand in hand with a shy boy,
under Neil Young's harvest moon.

But when I was a girl,
I did not see danger
in my teacher's gaze,
as I reached for his praise
and basked in his smile.

So when I grew up,
and unlocked the doors,
to find the empty roads in myself,
the ones that you make, unbidden,
I knew that I knew nothing at all.

The world remained a mystery still.
The word had failed to hold,
it couldn't stay death or give life to love.
And I knew not what I had done.
I knew only that the girl was gone.

Letting Go

ANIHO CHISHI

Pencil and ink on paper.

My Mother's Daughter

NEIKEHIENUO MEPFHÜO

It was my birthday today, but nobody knew. Not my friends at school, or anyone in my family. Only Mother would have remembered, but she was still in bed.

I longed for a blue dress to wear today, but I didn't want to disturb mother now. Later, I would draw myself a big cake on a piece of paper and colour it with all my favourite colours; just like I'd done for my younger brother and sister on their birthdays. There were five of us in our family including Father and Mother. I was the eldest among the children, so when Mother was not well, like today, I took care of my brother and sister. I used to love playing the role of mother, but these days I get really tired at the end of the day.

I didn't see Father that much, only at night. He was different from the fathers of my friends. He did all the things my friends' fathers didn't do. But I loved him anyway. Mother didn't speak that much and she had no friends. Except for the small smiles she gave us sometimes, I'd never seen Mother laugh. On the nights when Father came home, it meant either one of two things for us: one, pretend to be asleep, or two, hide under the bed. I felt we were a perfect family, but when Father was not home.

Last night was one of those nights when Father decided to come home. He hadn't been home in a week. As soon as I saw him walking through the gate, I quickly told Mother and hustled my younger brother and sister to bed and we pretended to be sleeping. Even my four-year-old sister now knows how to pretend to be asleep. I drew the blanket tighter over us and tried to control the shaking of my body as his footsteps drew closer. He opened the door to our bedroom and I joined my sweaty palms in a silent prayer that he would spare us tonight. He lingered there for a moment then slammed the door shut. We breathed out a sigh of relief, but we soon heard the muffled cries of Mother begging him to stop. And there we were, safe for the night but feeling terrified for Mother. I clutched my brother and sister close to me and we sobbed along to Mother's cries.

So today on my birthday I woke up at two in the morning to check on Mother. I switched on the light in the corridor, and from the doorway saw her sleeping, with a bloodied nose and mouth. I peeked into the living room where Father slept when he came home. It was empty. I went into the kitchen, made the fire, and put the kettle on. Then I mixed hot and cold water in a bowl and rinsing a clean cloth in it washed the bruises on Mother's face. She opened her eyes and weakly told me to go back to sleep but I carried on washing off the blood without saying a word.

When I finished, I asked, 'Why does he hate us, Mother?' and she quickly replied, 'No, child, he doesn't hate us. He was drunk, that's all. You know he does this only when he gets drunk at night. It's not his fault. It's because of the alcohol.' I didn't understand that, but I didn't ask for a clearer explanation. She was too weak and tired. I knew other men in our neighbourhood also drank alcohol, but their children and wives never had bruises like we did.

I went back to the kitchen to make sticky rice soup for Mother. She used to cook this for us when we got sick and now I had learned how to make it. My brother and sister woke up, so I put the kettle on again. They like their tea with a little snack, but this morning we hadn't any, so I put a spoonful each of last night's leftover rice into their cups. And then I began to cook rice and curry so that they could eat and get to school on time.

I dropped them off near the school gate. As soon as I saw them entering their classrooms, I ran back home. I was scared the teachers would see me. I couldn't be in school today as I had to look after Mother. I picked up the rice and curry I had kept aside for her in the kitchen, and went into her room to feed her. I sat quietly with her while she ate. To comfort her I said, 'We won't have to worry for some time now. You can rest. He won't be home for a few days, at least.' She nodded tiredly.

But he came home. This had never happened before. Usually, after, he stayed away for a few days. But, the three of us were sitting near the fireplace having our dinner when he suddenly showed up and we had no time to hide. Mother was still in bed. I looked up and froze seeing him. He eyes were like glass and I knew in my heart what he would do. He kicked away the plate from my hands, grabbed me by my sweater and threw me up against the wall.

'Father, I am sorry!' I cried.

He kept hitting me and finally I cried, 'Father, not today! It's my birthday!'

But, he didn't hear me.

I woke up in bed with my brother and sister sitting beside me and my mother gently washing the bruises on my face. I was relieved to find no marks on my siblings. It had only been me. I looked at mother and I began crying. Mother immediately pointed toward the living room and shook her head, her eyes sad. My crying would disturb him. If I woke him up, he would just get angry, again. So I turned my face into the pillow and muffled my cries.

At school the next day the teacher asked what had happened to my face. And just like Mother had told me, I said I slipped in the bathroom. I knew by the look in her eyes that she didn't believe me. This was the third time in a month that I had slipped in the bathroom. When she looked at me again, I looked away. They preached in church that if we lied, we would go to hell. But Mother always made me lie. Last time when Grandmother was visiting, I lied to her about the bruises on my forehead. I told her I hurt myself while playing with my friends. I was running out of stories to tell. So, I decided that the next time he hit me I would cover my face as much as I could, so that later on, there wouldn't be questions for me to answer with lies.

I'm lying in bed with my six-year-old daughter. I hold her close to me the way I once held my brother and sister on those nights when Father came home. I look at her sleeping face and wonder what she is dreaming about. I wish she could sleep peacefully like this, every night.

Then I hear heavy footsteps echo over the wooden floors of the house and once again, I find myself praying the same prayer I used to say many years ago, on hearing the footsteps of Father. I feel that same trembling in my body. My husband opens the door, and I shut my eyes wondering whether he will just leave, or reach for me. I can hear him standing at the door breathing heavily. Then he pulls my hair and yanks me out of bed, and drags me across the room. I stopped fighting back a long time ago. It only makes things worse, so I bear the blows. I am amazed every time. He is just like Father, and I am just like Mother.

I come to on the kitchen floor. The morning light streams into my eyes. I look around to find my daughter in the far corner, staring at me, just as I had looked at Mother years ago.

She runs up and lifts the hair away from my face and starts to cry, 'Why does Father hate us, mother?'

I raise myself up with difficulty to hold her. 'Shhh...child. Don't cry. Everything will be all right. He was drunk last night. It's not his fault. It's the alcohol in him that makes him do this to us.'

I gather my strength to stand and lift her up into my arms. I carry her into the kitchen, and with one hand, set some water on the gas stove to boil; half to make tea and half to wash with.

And when the water boils up, I will first wash and clean my daughter's face.

The Power to Forgive

AVINUO KIRE

She sat on bended knees, rifling through pages of old documents and other papers, some which would remain forever necessary and some which had long fulfilled their purpose. She had never been a particularly organized person. Mark sheets, old Christmas and birthday cards, and various outdated church programmes were all jammed inside a single brown cardboard file with the words 'Government of Nagaland', on the cover. A page of paper made a crackling sound of protest as she crumpled it into a ball and threw it towards the waste bin.

She was getting married soon. Sorting out her meagre belongings was the first phase of preparation for the new life she would soon embark upon. He had proposed a few nights ago and she had shyly accepted, like they both knew she would. She was twenty-eight and still retained youth's fresh-faced sweetness. He, on the other hand, was an unattractive man already well into his mid-forties; but she had no complaints. If anything, she was grateful that he had asked her at all. She had long resigned herself to the likelihood that marital life was not to be part of her destiny. Therefore, it did not matter to her that he was unemployed or that he could seldom hold his liquor. He had asked her to be his and that excused all his weaknesses. A feeling of affection overcame her as she recalled his uncharacteristic solemnity while discussing plans for their impending nuptials. 'I shall ask my elder brother and grand aunt to ask for your hand in marriage. You can tell your parents to expect a visit from my relatives this Saturday,' he had promised. To be treated so sensitively, as if she was as pure and untouched as any other sheltered young woman, touched her, endeared him to her. She was often suspicious when other men treated her likewise. 'Don't you know?' she would want to ask.

Shaking free from her habit of ruminating endlessly, she gathered the papers together and tapped them against the floor to align them. Upon that innocent act, a modest sized newspaper clipping suddenly slipped from within the pile and fell to the floor. 'FATHER FORGIVES MAN WHO RAPED DAUGHTER,' read the headline in bold capital letters. 'In a supreme act of Christian forgiveness…' began the report. But she did not have to read, did not need to. She felt the weight of the words even before they hit the smoothened mud floor. She had been acutely aware of this clipping while sorting out her papers and had been very careful to ignore it. Yet there it was, forcing her to confront once again, a single devastating memory that clung to her entire past like an overpowering rotten smell, effectively erasing all other remembrances. It seemed to her that memory was partial to pain and loss. A torrent of emotions: the old familiar wave of anger, shame and betrayal, a mind-numbing tornado of resentment that always left her with disastrous headaches, all these threatened to crush her happy mood.

She picked up the tattered newspaper clipping with distaste and tucked it beneath the mattress. She knew that she no longer wanted to preserve it in her file. At the same time, she could not bring herself to destroy it. A thought struck her as she resisted her immediate impulse to add the paper to the nearby trash. Perhaps it was quite natural for a person to form attachments to anything. One simply had to live with something long enough.

It happened sixteen years ago when she was only twelve. Her rapist had been her paternal uncle. Today, though other details had become vague with the passage of time, she still distinctly remembered the nauseating smell of him- a mixture of sweat together with a faint eggy sourness, and the hot wave of heavy panting. She recalled the agonising pain in the pit of her stomach which she had felt was ripping her body apart. The memory of it still made her wince to this very day. She was alone in the house and her uncle had left hurriedly after committing the heinous deed. He had murmured something to her before leaving but she could not remember what it was. A curious and kindly neighbour had forced her way into their neat three-roomed bamboo house and found her curled up in a corner, dazed and crying. Upon the woman's concerned probing, she had related what happened.

The little Naga village reacted in righteous uproar when the incident came to light. The story was reported in the local newspapers and various organizations voiced their fervent condemnation. Never had her little village received so much attention. She remembered her mother comforting her in the hospital while some police person wrote down her statement. She also remembered a group of women from some women's rights organization who came to visit her all the way from Kohima, the capital town. Her mother had made such a fuss over the women, and had related the horrific incident in detail, as though she had been a silent witness. This all happened a long time ago. She had known life before and after the unfolding of these events. It frustrated her therefore, how those few weeks often seemed to sum up the story of her existence. She avoided meeting new people. She had come to believe that they were the ones who would whisper behind her back, the ones who felt they knew her because of what had once happened to her body. 'There she goes, that's her,' they would say, 'That's the girl who was raped.'

Over the years, if not reconciled to it, she had learned to accept what had happened to her. There were moments she even forgot; happy times while gathering water or washing clothes beside the village river with other girls, when she imagined she was as carefree as any one of them. But such light-heartedness was always short-lived. 'People will think you have no shame!' Her mother was always quick to remind her. Mother never failed to lament the stigma that had become attached to their family because of her and at the same time, never encouraged anyone, her least of all, to revisit the incident. Mother had become a scared woman, always careful to maintain an emotionally detached relationship with her own daughter, fearful that intimacy would allow for indulgent exchanges. Though nothing was ever said, she sometimes felt that her mother blamed her for what happened. She sensed judgement through her mother's furtive glances, her thinly pursed lips, her grimaces, through the piercing gaze of narrow eyes. She thought no one understood the meaning of silences more than her mother; in time, she too had learned the language well. She would repeatedly agonise over the events which had unfolded that fateful day; over whether she ought to have been more alert, more wary, fought harder. But above all, her most agonising thought was whether life would have been simpler if she had kept that one day of her life a secret. She often wondered whether things would have been different had her mother discovered her first. Somehow, she knew she could get over the violation of her body; she could bear her shame in private. It only became intolerable when society 'shared' the shame.

She had been belatedly informed of her father's decision to forgive her uncle. A few weeks after the uproar had died down, her father came to her room and sat at the edge of her bed. He said so many things about forgiveness, justice and family honour. He said so much in such a grave voice. But nothing had prepared her for what he announced in the end. He stood up slowly as he spoke, indicating to her that his speech was nearing its end. With the air of parental authority, her father said:

'I have decided to forgive your uncle. But you need never worry about him; you will never see or hear from that man again'.

The taut stirrings of a strange and alien emotion bubbled deep within her at the words; feelings much too complicated for a child of twelve. Frustrated at not being able to express what she felt, she burst into helpless tears. Her father, a good but undemonstrative man, looked at her uneasily and said in a heavy voice, 'One day you will realize that this is the right thing to do. Hatred will only destroy us.' He said something about her uncle being in jail and also being excommunicated from their village. But nothing mattered more than her angry resentment towards her own father. She did not realize then, that the alien emotion she felt was betrayal. 'As if *he* had been the victim,' she would wondrously voice aloud to herself many times in years to come. That night, she had an especially vivid nightmare. In her dream, her uncle's giant face seemed pressed to her and she could not escape. She tried to scream but her voice died as the face of the enemy slowly morphed into her beloved father's wrinkled, worn features.

Sixteen years had passed since. Once a gay and cheerful child, she had now become withdrawn and reserved. She was still a dutiful daughter to her parents but it ended there. Her relationships with other people could be described as cordial at best. Though always polite, she was unable to forge close friendships. She had heard that her rapist uncle was now a free man. He had served seven years behind bars. Seven years in exchange for devastating her life. He had actually gone on to marry, have children and was now living with his family in Dimapur district. She bitterly wondered who had married him. She often broke out in a cold sweat whenever she came across anyone who resembled her uncle. Her biggest fear was the thought of meeting her uncle now, after all these years. This constant anxiety resulted in recurring nightmares. She knew it was unreasonable but she actually felt ashamed, even of him. As if she had played a role in her own disgrace.

Except for the youngest, all her other siblings – three sisters and two brothers – had married and relocated elsewhere. She was not particularly close to any of them. The one person in the world she truly held dear was her youngest brother, Pele. He was the only one who saw her as she was, without sympathy or judgement, without the shadow of what had happened to her hanging over her head. As incredible as it seemed to her, her sixteen-year old brother actually looked up to her as an elder sister and she loved him all the more for it. And now, she was finally getting married and soon to move out of the house she thought she was destined to live her remaining life and die in. A wry smile touched her face as she realized that she was like all women after all. Shifting required a sizeable amount of baggage, although in her case, the bulk of it remained unseen. It had become a part of her; she could not leave it behind.

'Your father will need a new suit,' her mother remarked. She looked at her mother contentedly picking stones out of the rice while helping her make plans for the wedding. It had been a long time since she had seen her mother so serene. She realized with sadness that she was not the only one who had changed. Her mother, once a warm and somewhat boisterous woman, had developed a quaint meekness, a pessimistic attitude so unlike the fearless woman she had once been. Her mother, she decided, had developed three different personalities: fierce towards her husband, long suffering towards her children and timid towards society in general. A long time ago, she had witnessed her parents quarrelling after a visit to her paternal grandmother. Eavesdropping through bamboo walls, she gathered that grandmother had blamed her mother for what happened to her.

'You stood there without defending me while your mother accused me of being a bad mother! How dare she blame me for our daughter's…!' her mother's angry tirade ended in sobs and she could not complete her sentence. Her father had replied, 'You are overreacting! She does not blame you, how could she? All she said was that mothers should be careful not to leave young daughters unattended!' Her younger self did not wish to listen anymore. She put little hands over her ears and faked sleep until it finally came.

Mother poured the cleaned rice inside an empty barrel, humming a soft lullaby while doing so. Her mother did not gossip. Perhaps she used to, but not anymore. She had too much at stake. 'We each have our cross to bear,' was her mother's ambiguous response to everything and anything unsavoury said about anyone. She sometimes pitied her mother's naivety in hoping that by not judging others, she would escape being judged herself.

Her silent reverie was broken by her mother's quizzical glance.

'Girl! Where is your mind, did you hear what I just said? Your father will need a proper suit to walk you down the aisle.'

She braced herself. She had been prepared for this issue.

'Yes of course. Actually, I am planning to ask Pele to walk me down the aisle instead of Father,' she replied tentatively.

'Nonsense! Your father should have that honour.'

'No, I want Pele to give me away, it's my wedding after all!' she stated firmly.

Her mother gave her a pained look but did not argue. She simply said, 'Think about it, your father will be very hurt.'

She felt a savage satisfaction at Mother's words.

Her brother Pele's reaction was predictable. 'Dear sister! Of course, I shall be honoured. But don't you think it should be Father?'

'I'd rather you do it,' she said stubbornly.

'It's your wedding,' he agreed.

She did not feel the same satisfaction.

Traditional wisdom discouraged long engagements, predicting that they gave rise to second thoughts and gossip. And so, a date was fixed quickly and it wasn't long before the wedding preparations began. The villagers arrived in droves to help; different groups for different work. The menfolk came together to construct a makeshift bamboo pavilion for the reception, and later helped to butcher two cows and a pig for the wedding feast. The women arrived to decorate the reception area and helped with the cooking and cleaning. The villagers felt good about being kind and generous to her; she was their tragic child. As for the bride to be, for all her cynicism, she experienced a renewed faith in human goodness. She found it overwhelming that all the fuss and hectic preparations were for her benefit. Also, her once antagonistic relationship with her mother had silently begun to heal of its own accord; the two women had never been as close as they were now. The stress and underlying tension of their relationship had begun to disappear ever since the night of her engagement. It was as if her becoming a bride had finally released her mother from her unhappiness.

The brief period of engagement was the happiest time in her life, so much so that she felt a sense of loss as the wedding date drew closer. The only thing that marred her happiness was the niggling unease that persisted whenever she thought of her father. He had calmly accepted that her brother would be walking her down the aisle but she knew he was disappointed. She was still his daughter, after all.

She knew that he was a good father and in other circumstances, she would have adored him. However aloof, he was an honest, hard-working man and provided for his family as best he could. An invisible barrier between father and daughter had been erected the night her father had informed her of his decision. It was the last that they ever discussed what had happened. She had been angry and resolutely avoided speaking to him the first few months, and he had let her be. In time, as she entered adolescence, she became too ashamed to ever broach the painful topic. In vain, she waited for him to take the initiative. Knowing her father's reclusive nature now, she realized it had been folly to expect that of him. So then, words which should have been spoken were bottled up instead, and it daily watered the seed of resentment sown deep within. In her subconscious mind, her decision to deny her father his right to give her away was her manner of punishing him for denying her the right to forgive a crime committed against her. Then again, when she saw his calm acceptance of her decision, she wondered whether he was all that affected by it. Had she managed to hurt him as deeply as he had her? It tormented her, this unfinished business. Finally, she resolved that she would tell him how she felt, how he had let her down. She decided to tell him everything, all her pent-up feelings. Only then would she find the peace that constantly eluded her.

She found an opportune time the evening before her wedding day. She had been sent home early to get sufficient rest and sleep for her big day tomorrow. Her mother, brother and the rest of her married siblings who had all arrived for the wedding with their families were still at the reception venue, making some final arrangements. She knew her father was alone at home. She carefully rehearsed her speech, the precise words to say and how to begin. Soon, she found herself approaching the house. Her rapidly beating heart compelled her to linger outside the front door for a while. She took a deep breath in order to steady her frazzled nerves. As she did so, a raw guttural sound from inside the house startled her. She quietly pushed open the door and stepped inside. Then she heard some inaudible words broken by fervent sobs. The sound came from inside her parents' bedroom. With her heart hammering in her chest, she looked inside the room, and what she saw made her freeze. Her weeping father sat awkwardly on a chair, elbows on his knees and hands supporting his bent head, revealing a mass of prematurely greying hair. Laid beside him on the bed was his new suit for her wedding and a rumpled copy of the church solemnization programme. She had never in her life seen her father show any strong emotion, let alone cry. It embarrassed and distressed her at the same time. She was not sure what to do.

Her father was unaware of her presence, and so she silently stepped back and retreated to her room. Feeling numb, she sat on her bed and tried to collect herself. She looked around the bare room, stripped of all belongings but for three pieces of luggage neatly stacked beside her bed. All worldly evidence of her twenty-eight years packed inside three pieces of luggage; a worn out VIP suitcase which had once belonged to her father and two colourful bags. One she had owned for some time, and the other was a wedding gift from her parents. She made a mental checklist of the things she wanted to take to her new life. Her soon-to-be husband had revealed a surprisingly kind and thoughtful nature during their time together. Despite his shortcomings, she knew that he could make her happy if she allowed him to. Her thoughts turned towards the tragic figure a couple of rooms away. Instinct told her that she was the cause of his profound grief. She closed her eyes and her body trembled. She knew then what she must do; for the first time, she wanted to do what she should have done a long time ago. Her right hand reached under the mattress and pulled out the newspaper clipping, cosseted for too long. For the first time, she felt no dread of the words staring back at her. She had encouraged herself to play the victim too long. It was now time to let go. She walked towards the kitchen and threw the incriminating paper into the fireplace. She did not bother to look as the flames consumed it in mere seconds.

With every brisk, purposeful step she took, the carefully constructed wall around her heart seemed to lighten; each brick loosened and crumbled, one by one. With a confidence she had never felt before, she pushed open the final door. Her father looked up and stood clumsily. He faced her unashamed, a grown man with tears and snot streaking his cheeks. They embraced and he kissed her forehead. In that loving act, the world of words mattered no more.

Tomorrow would bring yet another day and with it, new challenges. But somehow she knew now that she would be all right. She even thought about the fear that dogged her; the idea of accidently running into her uncle. This possibility no longer filled her with dread. In fact, she hoped she would meet him. She would hold her head high and look him in the eye. He would know that he did not 'ruin' her, that his evil had not tainted her. She revelled in the liberating absence of the bitterness which had long plagued her weary soul. For the first time since forever, she finally felt free.

First published in *The Power To Forgive and Other Stories* (Zubaan, 2015).

Untitled

LIMATOLA LONGKUMER

Micron pen on paper.

Rock

NINI LUNGALANG

My father slipped away in sleep;
He'd never agreed to die,
So he never knew he'd died.
For me, grief came late –
Long after the burial –
And I wept at last
For the bitter defiance
That refused to concede
The authority he'd claimed –
Something I would not yield –
And love's no substitute
For we were both hewn,
He and I, of the same
Rock
Flint strikes flint,
Anger seeks anger,
Ignites -
Burns. Burns. Burns.

But he slipped away
So I remain
Rock
Unforgiven, unforgiving.
I see his stern face
In death-sculpted
Austere waiting.
Wait, My Father, let
Your rage of living
Sear and scorch my heart
Till we wear down
Rock,
Erode time itself
Become an instant
Of flaming vapour
Startdust of eternity
Formless. Forgiving. Forgiven.

When Doors Open
A Personal Essay

EYINGBENI HÜMTSOE-NIENU

My mother was born in 1950, the sixth of seven surviving siblings, six of whom were girls. My grandfather, who had passed away before I was born, had not been happy about this. With every girl born in his household, his status and honour lessened, or so it seems he had thought. He was the priest of our old religious system. A small part of me wishes to give him the benefit of the doubt: maybe he wanted to ensure that the priestly line stayed in his family, although this was not a rule, but the greater part of me reasons that he already had a firstborn son as the most ideal successor. The gender of babies born into the family should not have mattered, but it did. He was clearly a patriarch first and a priest only after that.

The meaning of my mother's name, Loreni is 'line of girls' for she was the fifth daughter born in a row. As the third girl born in succession, my younger sister was wishfully named Lochumlo, which means 'the last girl'. It is no surprise then that under pressure from the patriarchal system, the girls in the community grew up to prefer having sons rather than daughters.

Grandfather had forbidden his daughters from going to school. He told them that they belonged to 'somebody else' (for they would get married and leave the household), implying that it was wasteful to labour in somebody else's garden! The other possibility was to attend the night school organized by the church on alternate days. Grandfather objected to that as well. He had been suspicious that receiving education in church would result in a change of faith in his daughters, and thus, the patriarchal instincts in him to keep the girls under his thumb intensified doubly. None of them was sent to school except for the one who, born prematurely, was physically unfit to do farm work. Much against her wishes, my mother too was forbidden from receiving a formal education. Her keenness to go to school was of no consequence and she had no option but to go to the fields every day. She was raised to obey the patriarch, and so she did, as did all her sisters. But, there was a female member in the family who dared to defy their father's autocracy. She was my mother's mother.

I got to know my grandma Njüponi as a little girl. Because she was born a female, grandma was given her name meaning 'one who is disliked' or simply 'unwanted', but I was very fond of her. She was caring and hardworking and smart, and a fervent believer in God. She converted to Christianity after grandfather died, and never missed going to church service even in her old age. Although she had nothing much to give, she was big-hearted and generous in spirit. She thought that if my mother wanted to go to school then she should.

Every evening, when most of the villagers were getting ready to retire, my grandma would carefully watch the door and quietly make all the arrangements so that my mother could sneak out of the house and attend night school at the church. Grandma's defiance of grandfather's rules, I believe, contributed much to her daughter's empowerment.

After a hard day's work in the fields and fetching water, manually pounding rice and cooking, my mother would run over to the church and learn how to read and write and sing Christian hymns. There were nights when after grandfather found out about my mother attending night school he would shut the door. On such nights, she would sleep on the *tsüngsa* outside the house. The next morning, she faced a harsh scolding, a fearful thing from a domineering figure. She attended three years of school in total. When she was in the third year, she received the academic excellence award in the school. Her prize was a hand-woven bamboo basket. She deeply cherished this token of her achievement. Unfortunately for her, this was the highest formal education she would receive. The night school was stopped for her; moreover by then she was a teenager. It was now time to 'knit the village' or *yanpi* as they say in our Lotha-Naga language. For a man though, it is meant as 'taking a woman' or 'building a house', *oki tssoa*.

My mother gave birth to nine children. Her first son was stillborn and she later buried another boy of seven. The second death broke her heart so grievously that I think it never fully mended. By the time she was thirty years old, my mother had already given birth to seven children. After losing two sons, she now had only the one son but alas, four daughters. This gender ratio was disappointing not only to my father but also my mother. Her motherhood, it seemed, was imperfect without more sons. After all, she, like most other women, mistakenly thought that the well-being of the patriarchal system and the continuity of her husband's lineage rested entirely on her womb's ability to produce males. She wrestled with God every day over the issue of granting her a son. However, yet another angelic looking girl was born to her.

Finally, at the age of forty-two, her wish was granted. She called him Pilamo, 'give back', for she thought that God had finally given back what he had taken away from her, a son. She now felt assured of receiving commendations from her village and tribe for birthing a perceived asset, a male, rather than a drawback, a female.

As a young girl, I questioned my mother's preference for sons over daughters but I never could confront her directly. She once told me why she felt that boys were more resourceful than girls: her older son, my brother, had managed to install a landline telephone in the house, an impossible thing then, and he could also drive a car. Although there were three daughters older than him, none of them could do either of those things. Her obsession for sons, it seemed, blinded her to the contributions of the daughters in sustaining the family.

Like most girls of her generation, who commonly viewed getting married as the ultimate goal, marriage came early to my mother and her sisters. But, her lower primary school education landed her a modest government job in Wokha town; quite an achievement for those days. She once confided in me that she was proudest of having economic freedom. She augmented her salary by rearing cows, pigs, chicken, fish, and growing vegetables of all kinds. Apart from their value as sources of food, she also 'saw' her children's fees in all of these creatures and plants. With the fruit of her labour, she was able to give tithe, support her children's studies and run the kitchen. She never ever bought things for herself. All of her life was meant only for giving, it seems. Her children never got the chance of offering her the fruit of her kindness through hard work of their own for, sadly, my mother died at the young age of fifty-nine.

I now know that the door which my grandma closely watched all those late evenings in the village enabled my mother to write letters in our Lotha-Naga language to her children who were mostly away from home for education. When I was in college at Jorhat, she once wrote to thank me for the gifts I had bought them with my post-matric scholarship. She especially mentioned the maroon polo shirt which I had sent for my father saying that she had teased him about how women would fall for him when he wore it! Her tough exterior concealed a soft interior. She was also able to write down her knowledge of folk songs, tales, and proverbs when I had asked about them. My grandma's bold action turned my mother into a successful homemaker and eventually into a woman of some stature in her community, proving that, for some women, all that it takes is an open door of opportunity.

I Wish You Were A Man

ABOKALI JIMOMI

Just as the seasons turn
Again and again they say to her
Again and again…
Woman, I wish you were a man
We could have been best buddies,
going out drinking, thrashing out issues, talking politics
Your ideas would be taken seriously.
If you were a man,
sounding real tough and loud you would be convincing
We could talk freedom fighters and illegal immigrants all night.
We could talk seriously about corruption and power abuse
Political and socio-economic issues?
That's a man's world to manage.
Woman, I wish you were a man

What you're saying actually makes sense
Your concern, discontentment, solutions; they feel right.
But, woman, you have no say

No matter how original and true your words.
Woman, you remain 'woman'
So talk about flowers and pigs, and clothes and shoes.
Woman, even women want women to know their place
Smiling, silent, simple-minded
So be
Where you are placed to be.
But if you were a man
You'd be you
Not an identity borrowed from your father or your husband
You'd be you
Voicing out what matters as a human, not merely a woman
But you're only a woman and that's the problem
We can't listen, no matter how wise your words
Woman, what a waste you weren't born a man!

I Just Hate
(A Performance Poem)

RŌZUMARĪ SAṂSĀRA

I don't hate my community of origin – Lotha-Naga
I just hate the patriarchy that suffocated me.
I don't hate my country of origin – India
I just hate how they always made me feel very small as a
tribal woman.
I don't hate my present home – Europe
I just hate how long years of Colonial Privilege have
blinded many into believing that they are a superior race.
I don't hate – Myself
I just hate how I gave power to all these forces to define my
life for so long.

NoNoNo Woman
(A Performance Poem)

RŌZUMARĪ SAṂSĀRA

The Naga nationalist told me to hate – the Indians
The Hindu nationalist told me to hate – the Pakistanis
The European nationalist told me to hate – the Immigrants
The American nationalist told me to hate – the Terrorists
I said NoNoNo – let me think for myself.

The Patriarchy socialized me to stay – an obedient woman
The Capitalist socialized me to buy – products after products
The Media socialized me to listen – to them and not to my
inner voice
The Womenfolk socialized me to serve – the Menfolk and to
forget myself
I said NoNoNo – let me think for myself.

Yes, I'm not your slave,
Yes, I'm not your toy,
Yes, I'm not your doll,

Yes, I'm not your so-and-so
Yes, what the hell!
I'M RŌZUMARĪ'!

And I'm a NoNoNo Woman.

Untitled

MARRIANE MURRY

Pencil on paper.

Shakto Chia
(Chang-Naga Folk song)

Translated by
ANUNGLA ZOE LONGKUMER

Male:	Over the earth are the bed legs
Female:	Over the bed legs is the bed frame
Male:	Over the bed frame are the bed boards
Female:	Over the bed boards is the woman
Male:	Over the woman is the man
Female:	Over the man is the woven cloth
Male:	Over the woven cloth are the roof joists
Female:	Over the roof joists are the rafters
Male:	Over the rafters is palm-leaf roofing
Female:	Over palm-leaf roofing is the thatch on the ridge
Male:	Over the thatch on the ridge is the bamboo ridge cap, and over that is God.
Female:	And over God is, woman.

Shakto means 'foundation' and the lines of this song are sung alternately between the man and the woman, with the woman cheekily having the last word. Collected from Hakchang village, Tuensang district, Nagaland. First published in *Folklore of Eastern Nagaland* (HPH, 2017), p. 175-176.

Outbooks
(A Personal Essay, September 2018)

NAROLA CHANGKIJA

During my high-school years, my mother made it very clear to me that there were only two kinds of books she approved of – the Bible, and my school textbooks. All other books were classified as 'outbooks'. This term covered any reading material that did not enhance my Baptist upbringing and experience or made me a better student.

Naturally, as a Naga girl growing up in the nineteen eighties and nineties, I wanted as many 'outbooks' as I could get my hands on. And wherever there's a need, someone turns up to cater for that need.

In Dimapur town, there were the tiny book-lending stalls, wedged in dark corners between shops, and run by entrepreneurial Indians who charged a minimal fee to lend every kind of book to every kind of curious Naga reader. As a schoolgirl with limited pocket money, these book-lending stalls catered to my hunger for real pulp literature. There was a roaring trade in Mills & Boon romance novels, as well as the saucier romance titles such as Harlequin and its ilk. Other popular items were Italian photo-romance magazines, British girl comics, Archie comics, Tintin, Asterix, The Phantom, Mandrake, and all the fashion magazines from the US and other Western nations, never mind that the issues were at least a year old by then.

Supplementing the so-called lending 'libraries' was a clandestine Mills & Boon network, where older cousins lent me their books, and I passed them around to my friends, or where I befriended the girls whose collections were more numerous than mine, or where we exchanged unread books with each other. It had never crossed my mind until later, to wonder why we Baptist girls sought out these books.

Was it for the tall, dark handsome white man who treated the blonde, brunette, red-headed, brown-haired heroine first with disdain and contempt, and then with inexplicable passion and romance? Was the fascination based on the strangeness and the exotic West?

We readers were nothing like the Mills & Boon starlets. We knew nothing about the world in those books: what champagne tasted like, how to wear an evening gown, what to say at a business meeting, how to swim in the waters near a Greek island, how to eat oysters, what a cocktail shaker looks like, or what the Tube was. We did not know this white world we read about, in our quiet bedrooms.

I know why I read these books – for the hot, naughty parts where the man makes furious, passionate love to the woman. I can't speak for the other girls, but I was still quite naïve. I didn't quite know how things fitted, but I suspected that it involved the parts *down there*. And so I quivered and touched myself, imagining it was happening to me.

But it wasn't enough. I went looking for something meatier and I found Abao's books. Sidney Sheldon and Harold Robbins and B-grade pre-feminist spy and detective novels that tore through the veils of polite language, and handed me the raw stuff – dick, oral sex, group sex, orgies, lesbian sex (*what?*), labia, vulva, chocolate up your poo-poo hole (*evil!*), women who say 'fuck me' and 'I want to fuck,' but are still happy and alive by the end of the story. (*And God didn't strike them down?!*) I read about all that with wide-eyed wonder.

When I consider the sheer variety of both pulp and crap, and quality literature that made its way to Nagaland, I am in awe of how things flow between cultures, where objects, materials, and people fly under the radar, across porous borders and checkpoints, bypassing censors and gatekeepers.

A kind of wild, wild east of pop cultural trade, appropriation, and piracy.

The perfect breeding ground for the kind of reader I am today.

But back then, I wasn't thinking such thoughts.

We were (I was) greedy for anything that showed us a world beyond Nagaland and Naga culture. We lived in a tribal world, a Scheduled Tribes world, where our internal realities clashed with our external state of being. We were the descendants of ancient head-hunters, but we were dependent on the generous funds of a Central Indian government. We were *not* like the plainspeople, the *tsumars*. But they were here, in the shops owned by Marwari businessmen, in the schools run by South Indian Catholic orders, and in the convoys of Assam Rifles army trucks rumbling down narrow mountain roads, or camped up on the hills of Kohima, or Phek or Tuensang, on the lookout for Naga insurgents.

Twentieth century modern life co-existed uneasily with traditional, custom-bound thinking and behaviour. Big-shot politicians and top cops would always be given the front row seats at the church on Sundays. Boys and girls from Youth Group would go on picnics near Chathe River in Chumukedima, but the flirting and the teasing were definitely borrowed from American teen movies. We would sing the gospels in church, while at home, we listened to Madonna and Michael Jackson, and I confess, Samantha Fox, mostly to annoy my mother. It was the same story, no matter one's culture or background – the need to escape, to enter other worlds than one's own.

It's interesting that I can't recall when I first learned to read a proper book. I certainly never learned to read the way some people claim, from the bedtime stories read by a parent to a child. Living in boarding school from the age of six doesn't allow for that kind of parent-child connection to develop. Also, I'd say my parents didn't really go for that kind of thing. Reading the daily Bible and saying our family prayers seemed good enough. In some childhood photos, there I am, age six, seven, whatever, clutching a bunch of thin hardcover books to my chest or holding up a comic book. Was I already able to read by then? Perhaps. I'm sure I liked looking at the pictures too.

But I would guess that I learned to read in boarding school. My memories of that school in Shillong are a mix of pleasant and not-so-pleasant images. But I remember, with some clarity, that this school had a tiny 'library'. If I try to describe what it looked like, I would say, with some imprecision, 'Imagine a corridor that runs from between the girls' dormitory and the boys' dormitory. Imagine that on one side of that corridor, are doors that lead to the principal's office and private residential rooms. Into which no one goes, unless you're really in trouble or there for piano lessons. Now imagine tucked into the other side of that corridor, one or two wooden cupboards with glass doors, surrounded by a handful of reading desks and chairs. Those desks and chairs were for the big boys and girls, in Class 10, and above, who were taught mostly by the principal. There were not many students in the higher classes, hence the small class was held in that corridor.'

It was probably there that I had my first encounter with 'outbooks'. Maybe it was a quiet Saturday, with students doing their own thing outside in the playground, or up in their dorms. All I know is that I found myself in that dark corridor, standing in front of the wooden cupboards. I remember being drawn to the silver/blue spine of a collection of fairy tales. I don't remember how I opened the doors and took out the book.

But I know that I laid open the book, on one of the senior students' desks no less, slowly turning one silver-edged page after silver-edged page, and revelling in the black words and colour pictures of Snow White, Beauty, Cinderella and all their kind...and the spell shattering when I looked up, and gazed into the eyes of a grim-faced principal, her cats-eye glasses glinting a little as the afternoon sun streamed in from a high window. The principal said nothing. I probably said nothing as well. I think I scurried away, fleeing for my life, abandoning the book at the desk. It was so long ago now; I must've been only eight – what did I know of how adults like her thought of children like me?

So much of my life has been marked by books, and by the ways these books came into my life. I suppose this is true of almost everyone who has grown up in the company of books. As much as I'd like to fancy myself as unique, I know I am very much the norm, very much the 'common reader'.

And yet, growing up in Nagaland, when it comes to books, to reading and writing, one can't help acknowledging that there are aspects peculiar or unique to a Naga place, time and context.

By the time my brother (age eleven) and I (age nine) were pulled out of boarding school, I had lost the ability to speak the dialect of my village Changki, and all I had left was English, some *Nagamese*, and a hunger to read. The first *proper* stories I read were Bible stories, about Noah and Moses, and Abraham and Isaac, and Ruth, and David and Bathsheba... in the colourful versions written for children. The Enid Blyton novels followed, along with The Hardy Boys and Nancy Drew mysteries. But in those days, Dimapur's only proper bookshop didn't have the most comprehensive stock. So, whenever Abao went to Delhi or Calcutta for police business, he took with him a list of titles I wanted, and I would wait in dizzy anticipation of his return home. Generally, he got home when I was at school or late at night, when I'd be asleep. But he never failed in his task. There they would be – new, colourful adventure stories that took me to a world full of English or American kids, either having adventures in magical lands or solving mysteries on desert islands, mysterious villages or remote caves, and eating marvellous things like jam drops, scones, burgers, and peanut butter sandwiches. Even their apples *sounded* tastier.

As a young reader, these are the only things that matter in the books you read. As an adult, you make note of the gentle ironies of a yellow-skinned tribal girl reading, nay worshipping, stories created by white authors now accused of racist and bigoted attitudes.

Still, it's not only the white race that is allowed to be bigoted and prejudiced. Growing up in a world that worshipped Billy Graham's brand of Christianity can do funny things to the tribal mind. Case in point – Abao's own naughty 'outbooks' that he probably never knew I had discovered and read. One day, I must have decided it was all too much. These were bad books, and I was a good Baptist girl. So one night, I collected all the Robbins and Sheldon books and burnt them in secret. It didn't matter that these were Abao's books, or that their fates weren't mine to decide – these were *evil* books and *must* be burned. Little did I know that, years ago, Abao had suffered a similar insult, when Alao burned a whole set of his Louis L'amour cowboy westerns because they were un-Christian books. For a year or so, I think I read only Christian-themed literature, and little Baptist pamphlets like *Why God abandons the heathen.*[1] The views in that one sat oddly with me. Something about it didn't feel right, didn't feel truly Christian or loving. Despite that niggling thought, I became an insufferable little Baptist, berating my male cousins for saying 'shit' and 'damn.' I went to Bible camps where I 'testified' for Jesus. At church youth services, I thundered out memorized Bible verses and sang with gusto in the youth choir. I was fully committed to being a young Baptist believer.

---

[1] Memory being what it is, I'm not sure if that's the correct title. A Google search leads me to the article 'Is God Unfair To The Heathen?' its author a pastor of a Baptist church somewhere in rural Minnesota, USA. Anyhow, the message is essentially the same – God abandons the heathens because they are born that way, and can never be saved.

Even if I continued to wonder why there were 'in' books and 'out' books, I was not intellectually fearless enough to make up my own mind. I tried, once...the day before my baptism, I announced that I wasn't ready to commit to Jesus and accept him as my saviour. I needed more time. The Youth Leader counselled me to continue with it, that it was better to make the gesture than to sit out the baptism. So, reluctantly, in bad grace, I got baptized in the Chathe River, and my ticket to heaven was stamped.

Eventually, something shifted, something changed. It was partly growing up, and partly that I just got bored reading nothing but Christian literature. And maybe Abao's hand was in there somewhere. For decades, he had subscribed faithfully to magazines like *TIME*, *National Geographic*, *Frontline*, *Newsweek*, even *Reader's Digest*, and he purchased all the various encyclopedias, thesauri, dictionaries, and condensed 'fiction' series that the Reader's Digest corporation would spruik to him, their most loyal consumer.

All these magazines filled the house and filled my mind with the words of people writing in the 'now', talking about the world we lived in, as members of a global community. It's clear now that Abao believed in 'outbooks'. How could he not, when they brought him glimpses of the world he lived in, with all its lurid and beautiful contradictions? How could he not yearn for more, when his job as a police officer in the Nagaland Police exposed him to the best and worst of human behaviour?

But these are just my imaginings about what my father may have thought. What matters is that his reverence for the written word was *catholic*, in the very best sense of the term. Literary or pulp fiction, any 'outbook' was evaluated and read and appreciated for its unique self. I like to think I have, finally, developed a similar catholic patience towards books, and life, and other human beings. At least, I hope I've learned how to value the things worth valuing and let the rest be. Abao's gone now, and Alao has held on to every scrap of material that evokes his memory and presence. So, it took a while before she cancelled the subscriptions to those magazines. And somewhere in the family library, are the old magazines, the old books, and other stubborn survivors of our mini book purges – they will ultimately go to better places, but not before I beg their pardon for being so rude to their fellow books, lost to time.

The Things I Told Me in 2017

DZÜVINGUNO DOROTHY CHASIE

The Tongue Tells More Than Tales

My tongue, as a child, was more adventurous than I.
It had more guts to try new things than I:
It turned orange with juice,
Turned pinker with sweets.
It got numb with things sour,
But didn't like bitter one bit!
But it taught me more than food, it taught me even more
It flagged me when I had no clue of how I felt:
So it was dumb in shock
Numb when I was ill
Wet when I was sad
And black when I would hate.
My child-tongue was much wiser than I.

Finding My Parts

Find me my parts and give them to me;
I've lost my valuable parts.
I have my hands, my arms, and my legs;
But something -
Something still feels like it's missing.

Self Portrait

BENI SUMER YANTHAN

You are Lotha woman, they said
Learn your father's language, and then your mother-tongue
The words hit hard the air in my family home
In suburban Dimapur.
So I drank the customary black tea with
Unfamiliar masculine grammar
In a town that burns the caustic sounds of my
mother's nostalgia
Looking every bit like the living memory of my Grandpa,
Kenes.

I have been told
I am a War
Between forgotten kisses of my father and
Sweat-soaked letters of my mother.
I come with an illegitimate handle to my body
And fidgety proverbs hanging on lips
Disentangle the deft movements
Of my foibles.

Commute

TALILULA

Let me internalize these roads.
Open cavities of filth and slush
Last night's leftovers on empty beer bottles
Cast-off sandals atop dirty diapers
Plastic heaps in motley hues.
Might as well, it seems
Since years of angry outbursts
And rallies and memes and parodies
All seem to have been in vain.

Every day from Dhobinalla to Rail Gate
Purana Bazaar, Padum Phukuri
2nd Mile, 3rd Mile, till 4th Mile
I hang on to the auto-rickshaw for dear life.

As we see-saw over potholes
And Charlie Puth croons softly in my ears
I re-arrange my scarf against the dust and stench

And try to tune out the ruin and decay of roads
And swallow my rising anger.
I think green hills, sunset and a chilled beer
Pork in bamboo-shoot for dinner
Far-off beaches, and clear blue skies and waters
Anything to avoid bad-road-depression.
And it works
Until the auto-rickshaw lurches to a halt
Next to a 'Do Not Throw Garbage Here' sign
Over a pile of litter.
Seems I've reached 4th Mile.

Martha's Mother

HEKALI ZHIMOMI

Seven-thirty in the morning and Martha and her mother were the first ones in line before the imposing gates of the home of the Minister of Public Works Department. Martha's mother stood fiddling with the latch on the gate, ready to run in the minute the gates opened for visitors.

'Mother, please don't touch that. The guard is looking at you.'

'Oh, let him,' her mother said, shifting a heavy bag bulging with fresh vegetables from Pfutsero to her other shoulder.

For the minister again, thought Martha. She had refused to carry the bag this time because she was ashamed – ashamed to be seen so eager to please and to be seen buying people's favours by plying them with all sorts of gifts. Her mother, on the other hand was neither the kind to be ashamed nor the kind to give up easily.

This was the fifth time they were visiting the Minister. Not to count the many visits they had paid to other important people in the Government because Martha's mother was determined to get a government job for her only daughter.

Martha herself did not nurse such ambitious dreams for herself. Having given up her studies after passing her tenth grade, she had thrown herself into a flurry of church activities. In their neighbourhood she was known as the quiet, pretty girl who helped out at Sunday school. Her virtues were praised, more so because her father was infamous for his drinking and gambling.

Her mother, however, was feared by everybody in the colony. She was the President of the local women's unit and a member of almost all the committees that were set up in the colony. She spoke her mind and other people's too and was not someone you could take lightly.

She had often led the women of the colony in raiding the liquor dens. Never mind the fact that most of these women were married to drunkards who beat them, silenced them and destroyed their peace of mind. In turn, they spewed out their anger on those who sold liquor to their men, hurling bottles of liquor out from the den, upturning their brewing pans and pulling out the young girls who served liquor onto the street.

Yes, Martha's mother was quite a prominent citizen, having been pictured quite often in the local dailies, standing proudly with her colleagues before an assortment of liquor bottles and pots of local brew. She actively took part in politics and everyone knew that in the Municipal elections, she had voted at least forty times, making good use of a small bottle of hydrogen peroxide.

The local boys were afraid of her and so no matter how pretty Martha was, she had no suitors calling at her door. You could say that at twenty, Martha did need not to bother about not receiving any marriage proposals, but the truth was that she did.

Her friends were all married and were busy nursing babies, washing buckets of clothes and cooking endlessly and Martha, denied a 'normal' family life, wove dreams of similar domestic scenes for herself. And that was also the reason why Martha was clearly not happy about meeting the honourable Minister of the public works department for a job. Working mindlessly at a desk in some dusty office did not quite feature in her many dreams.

The line before the gate kept growing and visitors started getting restless.

'When will we be allowed in?' barked an old lady from the back.

'*Arre*, how should I know,' replied the guard standing at the gate.

'The Minister-saab must be busy.'

'Busy? Looks like they are still sleeping at this hour,' retorted the old woman.

Martha turned around to look at the old woman and caught a familiar face smiling at her. Ah, the boy she had met last month while waiting to meet the Minister of Soil Conservation. Vethole, he had said his name was. He too had been dragged by his father to request the Minister for one of the Government subsidy schemes. Vethole had mentioned to Martha that he worked at the local Airtel office at Chumukedima and had cheekily asked for her number. Martha didn't own a mobile but rather than admitting this, she had told him she was not in the habit of giving her number to strangers.

And here he was again, beaming at her over a sea of heads. Martha returned the smile and quickly turned before her mother caught the clandestine exchange.

Someone from the house shouted and suddenly the guards swung into action. The rusty hinges screeched and gave way as the guards opened the iron gates just enough to let the visitors in one by one. The queue broke as visitors struggled to squeeze in through the space, pushing each other aside. From then on, it was a hundred metre dash into the waiting room adjoining the Minister's camp office.

Martha's mother, as usual, was the first in. Martha hung back a little and as expected, she heard Vethole say, 'Again, we meet.'

They exchanged quick looks. They were conscious of the people around who watched them curiously as they had nothing better to do while they waited their turn.

'What are you here for today?' Martha asked him quite formally.

'My father is trying for a small post at the Engineer's office. I don't even know if there is any vacancy but the old man insists that the Minister can help.'

'Post for whom? Your father?' she asked.

'For me, who else?' he said with little enthusiasm. 'By the way, where did you say you lived?'

'You know very well I didn't tell you last time. I stay at Signal Bosti near the bakery.'

Suddenly, Martha's mother appeared. 'There you are! Come on, hurry, we can't keep the Minister waiting!' she said and dragged her through the crowd into the office of the honourable Minister.

A fair and stocky man, he sat chewing *paan* as he listened.

Martha's mother lavishly praised the Minister about how well his department was doing and how well his officers and party men spoke of him.

Martha cringed in embarrassment for her mother as it was clearly obvious that the Minister was keen to get rid of them. He did not bother to ask them to sit. Unable to speak with his mouth full of *paan*, the Minister gestured for the application in her mother's hand. He wrote something almost illegible, signed with a flourish and then said, 'Give this to the Engineer. He knows what to do.'

'Please Sir, write there specifically for a job for my daughter,' Martha's mother pleaded.

The Minister smiled and said, 'Since when have you people started telling me what to write?'

'You are our Minister, what can I say! But sir, I have also worked so hard for the party. And you know about the forty votes I cast last elections…'

The Minister interrupted and said, 'I know, I know, and that is why I tell everyone you are such a good party worker! Here take this.'

Martha's mother took the application and saw 'Special Case' written on the paper with a signature scrawled generously across. *Paan* stains now dotted the application, affirming the Minister's preoccupation.

As the two left the room, Martha's mother left the bag full of vegetables discreetly at the side of the door saying, 'Memsaab likes her vegetables fresh so I bought a little something for her from Pfutsero.'

The Minister smiled and feebly protested saying, 'You shouldn't have.'

With that, they stumbled out of the office into the waiting

room where other visitors were anxiously waiting for their turn.

Martha sought out her friend and catching his eye, smiled at him. Before she could say anything, Martha's mother pushed her out of the door. Once out, Martha's mother fished out the application from her bag and read out the Minister's note. She was afraid to say anything, not quite sure what to make of the 'Special Case' written on it.

She glanced at Martha and sighed and said, 'See, what I have to do for you.'

'Please Mother, don't start. I didn't ask you to do anything for me.'

'Don't be ungrateful. You will thank me for all this one day.'

'But, I'm not interested, Mother,' Martha protested.

'So, what are you interested in?' her mother asked.

'I don't know,' she replied miserably. She wanted to say she didn't really know much of anything to decide what her interests were. What with Father constantly drunk and you busy in all your rallies, party meetings and fighting social evils, where do I find time to learn about the world around me, she wanted to say.

Instead, she simply said, 'Mother, let's go home.'

Her mother looked at the letter in her hand and hesitated. Finally, she said, 'All right, enough for today. In any case, I have nothing to give the Engineer. Tomorrow, I shall get a leg of pork. I need to borrow money from your aunt Chumbeni. Let's go.'

The next morning Martha's mother got up at the crack of dawn. Her husband lay sprawled, snoring, and reeking of alcohol. His belly spilled over the blanket and spit drooled into his pillow. She didn't have time to change out of her nightdress so she hurriedly washed her face and combed her hair, coaxing it into an untidy bun. Glancing at the mirror she let out a sigh as she saw the dark circles under her eyes and the pigmentation on her cheeks spreading like a dark stain on her face. She had been so busy with party meetings and running around for Martha's job and had not been getting enough rest. A small and sturdily built woman, she had never suffered any chronic health problems but on a visit to a local doctor last month, she had been diagnosed with hypertension.

The cause for it all, she thought viciously, was that no good husband of hers. If only her husband had offered her and her daughter a better life. She walked over to the bed and yanked at her husband's pillow. His head rolled onto the bed but he did not wake up. She quickly slipped her hand into the pillow cover and took out a small bundle of ten rupee notes. She barely glanced at her husband, a stranger to her now. A loser, that's what you are, she thought. You gave up trying for yourself, for me, and our daughter, but I won't allow that to happen to me, she vowed silently.

Without waking her household, she slipped out and walked down to the butcher's shop at the junction. There was already a small crowd around the butcher, haggling for the choicest portions. But they made way for Martha's mother for there was not a single person in the colony she hadn't helped or fought against.

'This leg here,' she said. 'How much are you asking?'

'Aunty, for you only a hundred per kg,' the butcher replied.

'*Arre*, it was only ninety-five the other day, what happened? The pig traders on strike again?' she asked, jabbing the meat with her forefinger.

'It's fresh, aunty, don't you trust me? Here, I'll add this piece of liver and fat and it's all of five kgs. That's five hundred rupees, aunty.'

'That is too much. Reduce the rate or I will have your weights checked again.'

'Now, why do you have to talk like that? See, I'll even add this extra piece of tailbone so please don't ask me to reduce any further. If I don't earn a little profit, why would I be standing here selling meat?'

'Oi, I want extra pieces too. The Board of Deacons is having a meeting at my house this evening,' yelled out a woman from the back. Martha's mother recognised her neighbour Aholi.

'For my friend too. Be generous today. People like us don't buy meat every day.'

'What are you saying? If you don't eat meat who will? Can we survive without pork?'

The butcher packed her portion in a black polythene bag and handed it to her.

Martha's mother hurried back to find her household still asleep. The servant boy was still snuggled up in his makeshift bed near the television. Her husband could be heard snoring. She knew he would be up at noon for his lunch before he started his daily round of drinking. But Martha's room was still shut and that was unusual.

Martha's mother rudely jolted the servant boy out of his sleep by throwing off his blanket and then knocked on Martha's door.

'Get up Martha. We have to catch the Engineer before he leaves for his office. Don't bother to bathe or we'll be late,' she shouted. But there was no reply and she banged on the door.

Puzzled, she looked down to find the door was latched from the outside. She gingerly opened the door and stepped into Martha's tiny room.

As tidy as ever, her daughter had neatly made her bed and on it Martha's mother saw an envelope.

It was addressed to her. She slowly picked it up, opened it and read, 'Mother, I'm sorry to disappoint you, I don't think I would like to work in some government office. I hate meeting people and begging for jobs. I met a boy I like and he proposed to me last evening. His father has got a government subsidy scheme or something like that for him. We'll be all right, so don't worry about me. We'll come back and meet you when you are no longer angry. Please give us your blessings. Martha.'

Martha's mother slowly put the letter down and walked out of the room in a daze. She could hear the beating of her heart. Thud, thud, thud, it went, louder than the clock in her kitchen. Unsure of what to do next, she sat down on the wooden stool near the television. Muddled thoughts ran through her head.

What would people say now? She would have to resign from her membership in the church and as the President of the local women's unit of the colony and what shame she would have to bear!

She sat trying to think clearly. Her husband, now a stranger to her, and the servant boy could hardly share in her shame and humiliation. Just then the doorbell rang and the servant boy let in the unwanted visitor.

'Aunty Aholi is here,' he announced unnecessarily as her visitor sailed in oblivious to the turmoil that was setting in.

'Please, please can Martha help me out this evening? I don't have anybody to help me with the cooking for this evening's dinner. All fifteen of them, I tell you, I am worn out with all these meetings and dinners. Where is Martha?'

'Martha? Oh, Martha, don't you know?' the mother replied as calmly as she could. And she found herself saying, 'That girl of mine, as considerate as ever. She did not want to trouble her father and me over wedding expenses. So she has left with that nice boy of hers.'

'Boy? Eloped you mean?' shrieked her neighbour.

'No, of course not,' Martha's mother replied, her fist tightening around her daughter's letter in her pocket.

'I gave her my prayers and blessings. That drunken father of hers has no money for her wedding, so we talked about this. Why waste money over silly wedding arrangements? Why, I myself told her to leave before her father makes some silly objection.'

'But, who is this boy? Surely she could have told us.'

'My Martha, you know how quiet and shy she can be. I knew, of course. The boy is too good and besides, he is working on some important government scheme. I will tell you everything later but hush now, my husband will wake up.' With that Martha's mother gently pushed her friend out.

At the door, she called out, 'Save your congratulations for later on when I invite the couple back. Why do you think I bought the pork this morning?'

With that, she shut the door on her visitor.

First published in *Of Voices And Paper* (Ed.Susan Waten, *HAWA*, 2009), p. 7-13.

Vili's Runaway Son

ABOKALI JIMOMI

Madam Ela was busy in her kitchen, making her morning cup of tea, when Vili showed up at the front door, with her tale of woe. She needed money, in order to save her husband and son from the No. 2 underground faction.

Madame Ela was a government primary school teacher who earned a small salary which she supplemented by rearing pigs. She was a stern and enterprising, but also generous, woman. So when Vili climbed all the way up the hill to her house to beg for her help, Madam Ela sat Vili down and started making more tea.

'Madam, both my son and husband will die if I don't save them! Please help me get the money!' Vili begged.

Vili was forty-two, and had lived in this small town since the age of five. Both she and her husband were daily-wage workers, doing odd jobs in town people's houses; he sometimes fixing broken windows and doors, or pruning trees, and constructing pig pens and cleaning water tanks, and she collecting pig fodder and weeding vegetable gardens.

Tearfully, she described how the night before, way past midnight, two men armed with AK-47 rifles had forced open the wooden door of their home and entered their bedroom. Despite her pleas, the men tied her husband's hands at the back, blindfolded him, and took him away. Vili now had just a week's time to raise the princely sum of two lakh rupees that the underground faction demanded for her husband's return.

There was a reason for all this, Vili explained to Madame Ela, looking shamefacedly down at her cup of tea. Four years ago, her son had dropped out of school. He hadn't been seen since. She had heard that he had joined the No. 2 group along with some other boys from the colony. And then just last week, Vili got news that he ran away and joined another group, stealing something called an SLR gun which cost two lakhs, and because of that, her husband was taken away last night. Since her son was now seen as a betrayer, it was protocol that his parents and relatives compensate for the loss.

'How on earth will I get two lakhs of rupees to save my husband?' she moaned. 'Madam, please help me, there is no one I can turn to.'

Madam Ela knew Vili's family was a helpless and hopeless case. None of them had full-time jobs. Her husband was a cough syrup addict who rarely worked. Only Vili's earnings ran the household but even she herself did not seek a regular job. She came only two times a week to her house to collect pig fodder.

Their son had dropped out of the Government High School in class eight and joined the gang of school drop-outs from the colony. The gang would roam about town all day doing nothing much. Their main preoccupation was collecting leaves from the weed plants that grew along the roadside or in backyard gardens. When dried, they would crush the leaves, roll them in strips of paper and smoke them up. Sometimes they would cut lengths of telephone cables to sell to the *luhatina* man, and with the money buy bottles of cough syrup. Like all the other kids, their son too had demanded a smart phone and a pair of player-boots, but they could least afford things like that, unlike the other parents.

'*Aya*! This is such a mess. Who can we blame? What will become of your son, and hundreds of other children like him who have dropped out of school and have nothing meaningful to do?' Madam Ela said this more to herself than to her guest. There was silence for a few moments as the two women sipped red hot tea from Madam Ela's white enamel mugs.

'What about your son?' Madam Ela asked. 'Why don't you ask him to come back and surrender?'

'He'll be shot dead if he comes back! But I can't even contact him...,' Vili sobbed, pressing her hands on her chest, trying to suppress the stabbing pain she felt there.

'Vili, I don't have that kind of money. I wish I could help but...,' Madam Ela began gently.

'We have run out of options! This is the curse of our times! This is Satan's work!' Vili whispered fervently. 'I just need money! I'll sell the two pigs I have, and if you could, let me sell some of your pigs! I'll help feed more pigs later, in repayment!'

'Hmm, one of your pigs will fetch you at least twenty thousand,' said Madam Ela. 'Now that the festival is just around the corner, it sounds like a workable plan to sell the pigs.'

After some deliberation, Madam Ela decided, 'I'll give you one of my big pigs. In return, you can collect pig fodder for the next six months. Even though the amount from selling the pigs is not going to be enough, you could always try and negotiate with the underground. Explain your situation to them.'

Vili went home feeling a little better.

That night, Madam Ela sat on the chair in her verandah for a long time. There was no moon out. Only the outlines of dark rainclouds showed faintly in the sky. The neighbourhood was quiet except for the tall bamboo rustling in the breeze, swaying over the tin-roofed bamboo houses looking like ghostly apparitions hovering, waiting to pounce on someone. She shivered slightly and went inside.

That night, Vili sat by the fireplace in her kitchen crying, remembering how the men had pushed her husband into the vehicle and how they had driven away, the red backlight of their Maruti Gypsy swiftly receding in the dark.

Who would give her such a large amount of cash? She had nothing valuable to sell or mortgage. The police or the government would not touch her case, and even if they did, it would take years before anything came out of it. What if both her husband and her only son never came back? Vili felt weak and helpless. Who would help her? As it was, her family was living hand to mouth.

The sun rose bright in the sky and yet Vili felt no warmth. But, taking a deep breath, she resolutely got up and headed out for the marketplace to sell the pigs. With the money from selling the pigs, Vili then went to meet up with the Commanding Officer of the group that had taken her husband.

'Please sir, I've got some money today. It's not the full amount but this is all I could collect for now,' Vili said. 'Please in the name of God, let my husband go!'

To her horror, the Officer responded with fury. 'That's not enough! No money? No gun? No negotiations. It's our policy. Your husband is going nowhere until you get your son and the gun, or the money.' They were all seated inside a log house, Vili and the Officer, while her husband was in a corner, flanked by two guards.

'Where is your son? Where are your relatives? Ask everyone you know, your officer-relatives in town, *they* can help you with the money at least. I can't do much, even if I wanted to. A rule is a rule,' the man said impatiently.

'I have no news from my son! I don't even know where he is! I don't have any rich or powerful relatives!' Vili cried.

'In that case, this will teach you all a lesson,' the Officer said, removing his belt with the heavy brass buckle from around his waist.

He pushed her husband outside.

'You must have instructed your son to turn against us!' he accused Vito, lashing him with the belt.

Vili cried out, 'Please! Please sir! Please don't hurt him. I will ask all my relatives to search for my son! Please sir, please don't hurt him!'

She tugged at the officer's shirt, 'Please sir! Give us one more chance!'

'Do you see that post there?' The man pointed to a house pillar. 'We will tie him there and give him a hundred lashes every day, till you get the money, or the gun. Now go,' he shoved her away from him, 'before I do the same to you!'

Terrified and helpless, Vili risked one last despairing look at her husband who lay crouched on the ground, moaning in pain. Then she fled the place, and hurried all the way back to town, to call on her family relatives. All day, she went from house to house, begged all her relatives and all her neighbours for help, but no one could give her that kind of money.

In the end, she retraced her steps to Madame Ela's house, crying, 'No one can help me, Madam. Only you can help me! God will repay you abundantly even if I can't! Only *you* can do something for me now!'

Madam Ela was torn between helping Vili and putting up her hands and saying no, frustrated with the futility of human predicaments such as this.

Who gained anything from out of all this? What price to pay, for a stupid gun? Why did her son run away? Why did they even bother to have children? Why couldn't they get a proper source of income?

'There's no solution in thinking so much!' Madam Ela grieved and took a loan of fifty thousand rupees from her Self-Help-Women's Group and gave it to Vili who, encouraged, went to the local politician, the headman of the colony, and the money lenders, and collected the cash she needed.

After much running around, one of her relatives negotiated with someone who knew someone who worked with the higher-ups at both the No. 2 group and the No.X group her son had joined, and a settlement was reached. Her son was tracked down and the gun handed back to the No. 2 group along with the two lakhs.

'Let's go home,' Vili said to her silent husband, on the day when he was finally released.

It had taken her two months of going back and forth between the town and the underground camp before her husband was released. In that time, he had received lashings for every day that the money was not forthcoming. His body was scarred and bleeding from the daily punishment inflicted on him, and he could barely walk anymore.

It had rained heavily earlier that day and the afternoon sky was now clear and bright. In the distance, the ranges of green mountains circling the town now looked blue and seemed to stretch into infinity.

As they both staggered into the house, Vili's thoughts raced, thinking of the months ahead when she would have to collect pig fodder for Madam Ela, and do whatever else possible to pay for her husband's medical treatment and repay their debts.

'Who fixed the door?' her frail husband asked.

'I replaced the twisted hinges, it wasn't too difficult,' Vili smiled.

She ignored the pang in her heart, thinking of her runaway son.

Outside her window in the small backyard garden by the wooden pigsty, rain-washed umbrella-like yam leaves and green bean plants were growing bigger and greener.

Advertisement

BENI SUMER YANTHAN

Come beside me, lover
In this town neither happy nor sated
Where blasphemies are swallowed down with every rum shot
And causes burn on behalf of martyred ideologies
Where desire gets hollowed out in a hotel room
And its guts spilled out in these dull streets
I'll give you a little bootlegged drink
If you want the smell of night.

Come, my friend, in this place
If you want to
Carve out the addendums to their lies
Note the invaders' sirens blasting through the night

If you want to
Look in men's pockets loaded with curfews
And the fragrances of women pinned to full-length coats
Wake and startle to the soft bellows of orchids

I'll give you a little bootlegged drink
If you want the smell of night.

Come here, right now, stranger
Under the sheath of ether shielding this long delightful night
But, never can you
Claim the silences drawn out in the darkness
Like in stars with the force as they do
No quip flounce down your lips
No lover's wail rend through the soft underbelly of this
amorous town
Like precocious syllables prematurely spilled
They'll count for nothing.

What Time Told Me in 2018

DZÜVINGUNO DOROTHY CHASIE

Kind of Perfect

My hands are empty,
And kind of cold.
So I've introduced them
To the company
Of itchy pockets.

But I know
They'd rather be
Somewhere else,
Both in warmth
And in company.

It is like punishment,
In all good reasoning,
For not grasping onto
What it awed at
Once so giddily.

I know
There is nothing more
That can be said or done,
For those hands lie
Blue and stone.
But I know somewhere;
For I've seen it in my dreams.
These hands and those,
Stay warm and held;
Almost -
Almost perfectly.

Secret Library

Stacks of books and fat binders
Live inside the inside.
Piling up and up
Like the years long and wide.
The torn and dusty
From neglect,
Live in the same space
As the fresh and pulsating new.
Some sections neat,
Others rundown and caved-in
But that's like the beauty
That comes with the beast.
And way beyond the
Millionth row
And past the five hundredth fifty-fifth aisle
You will see me tearing, wiping, re-reading, in mounds
As well as adding in the new.

Odyssey

T. KEDITSU

Leave this place, travel all you want
Wander the world and even settle there
Your blood will always be of this land.
Don't you know? The womb that held
You is buried here inside our earth.
Placenta of generations still bright red,
Throbbing with the ache of birth
Have fed our soil from the time

Our ancestors were supple stones.
And you wonder why, having left
You can never pry the core of your being
From the grasp of this land.

This land drenched in the blood
Of our birth is midwife
To our forests and gardens
She nurses the tart roselle,

Suckles the trusty taro, weaving fabrics
Of clouds and rain that
Bathe our terrace fields into fecundity;
She adopts foreign freesias
And long ago, fed the chilli,
Bred by sanctified Aztec blood,
Weakened and famished from its travel
Across seas and continents
With the blood of equal warriors
To create terrifying sweetness
That sears nerves into ecstatic submission.

The language of blood is not song,
Singing like sirens atop seas
Of dying ancient forests and crumbling rock.
For then we would just plug our ears,
Sail on, scarred but free.
No, blood is not even language,
It runs in us, through and out of us
Cousin to iron that churns in the molten core
Of our earth and orchestrates
Our seas, our skies, our seasons;
And when this blood that birthed you
Is returned to its kin, you are merged
Forever to this land, creating an axis
That draws you in, even as it lets you
Run, reeling in your spirit
To roots you would shun
So escape, wander, try and forget.
For wherever you die, far away,
Buried, burnt, drowned,

Or falling with melted wings from the sky,
Our land will claim you back.
The blood of your mother will return
You to the blood of the One who birthed us all,
Hunched over her loom, weaving
And unravelling her weft ceaselessly
Waiting for your homecoming.

In leaving, you will learn your place.

Untitled

MANENJUNGLA AIER

Watercolour on paper.

A Fairytale Like Any Other

THEJKHRIENUO YHOME

Notes on Authors and Translators

ABOKALI JIMOMI is a writer, entrepreneur and mother. Since 2011 she has been running an organization called Organic Nagaland, supporting local produce from Nagaland and promoting organic food, as well as networking with women self-help groups and women farmers.

AHIKALI SWU graduated from Miranda House, Delhi University. She compiled and translated a collection of Sumi-Naga poetry and released a book, *A Glimpse of Long Ago: Sumi-English Folk Poems* (2014). She is a mother of three and lives in Dimapur, Nagaland.

ANIHO CHISHI is a young budding designer and artist who feels it is important to show one's identity and feelings through one's work. The sense of freedom and expression drives what she does, and is, for her, also an escape from the hustle and bustle of life, and something through which she can express things even better in words and actions. The type of art she practises reflects the person she is, and she feels that every individual needs a platform to show who they really are. She tries to stay true to what she believes in and show what she sees in her mind through the medium she has chosen.

ANUNGLA ZOE LONGKUMER can best be described as a free individual discovering her way through creative pursuits in music, writing, filmmaking, and folk traditions. Having travelled and lived outside Nagaland for most of her life she is currently based in Dimapur, Nagaland, where she freelances doing some content editing, music, and filmmaking, and is involved in ongoing research in folklore. She has authored a book *Folklore of Eastern Nagaland* (2017) containing translations of folktales, folk songs and real life accounts collected from the six tribes who inhabit the more remote districts of Eastern Nagaland.

AVINUO KIRE is a writer and teacher from Kohima, Nagaland. She has contributed to various literary journals and magazines and has authored three books; an anthology of short fiction stories titled *The Power to Forgive and Other Stories* (Zubaan, 2015), a collection of poetry *Where Wildflowers Grow*, and has co-authored a collection of documented oral narratives titled, *Naga Heritage Centre, People Stories: Volume One*. Avinuo is currently Assistant Professor of English at Kohima College, Nagaland. She continues to write and is presently working on her next book.

BENI SUMER YANTHAN: Born to a War-Jaintia mother from Meghalaya and a Lotha-Naga father, Beni has led a somewhat peripatetic life, having moved from Nagaland to Bangalore, Delhi and Hyderabad. She is passionate about literature, art, music, travel and the oxford comma. When she is not scheming of ways to meet as many cats as possible, she can be found tweeting about her favourite football team, Arsenal, who no one really cares about. She considers herself an accidental academic.

DZUVINGUNO DOROTHY CHASIE is currently employed as Guest Faculty in the English Department at Nagaland University, Meriema Campus. She has completed her M.Phil in English and aims to pursue further research. She has been composing poetry and short stories since her school days, and took up spoken word poetry during her Masters as an additional tool to exercise creativity and spread messages of understanding, peace, and empathy. She believes that writing and creative public-speaking are important tools that still have the potential to grow in her home-state of Nagaland. She wishes to encourage her peers to partake in this journey of self-awareness and self-expression.

EASTERINE KIRE is a poet, short story writer, children's book writer and novelist from Nagaland. Her first novel *A Naga Village Remembered* (2003) is also the first Naga novel written in English. In 2011 she was awarded the Nagaland Governor's Award for Excellence in Naga Literature. In 2013 she was awarded the 'Free Word' by Catalan PEN, Barcelona. In 2015, her book *When the River Sleeps* (Zubaan, 2014) won the Hindu Literature Prize. Her book *Son of Thundercloud* (2016) was awarded the Tata Book of the Year in 2017, and the Bal Sahitya Puraskar in 2018. Her work has been translated into German, Norwegian and Marathi. Easterine Kire holds a doctoral degree from the University of Poona.

EM EM EL is a teacher and a lover of words who has been based in Illinois, USA for the past eleven years. Faith, food, family and friends are the driving forces that fuel her to live boldly, and love fiercely, with an intention to engage with the world through her writing.

EMISENLA JAMIR is a writer from Kohima, Nagaland. Her short story *'Deliberate Delirium'* was published in an anthology of short stories titled *Raconteurs from the Hills* (2014). She has also co-authored a collection of women's poetry titled *Woven Words* (2017). She is currently working as Assistant Professor of English in Kohima College.

EYINGBENI HUMTSOE-NIENU is a Senior Lecturer at Clark Theological College, Mokokchung, Nagaland. She teaches Christian Doctrines and Feminist Theologies. She has written several articles for Christian journals and books, including an award-winning article, 'De-masculinizing God: Reclaiming the Inclusive Meaning of God in Tribal Tradition'. Among few others, she is the author of *God of the Tribes: Christian Perspective on the Naga Ancestral Idea of the Supreme Being* (2014), and co-author of *Nagas: Essays for Responsible Change* (2012).

HEKALI ZHIMOMI is an IAS officer from the 1996 batch and is currently posted as Secretary to the Govt of U.P. Medical, Health & Family Welfare Department. She is also M.D., Uttar Pradesh Medical Supply Corporation, Lucknow. She served as the first woman Deputy Commissioner of Dimapur district, Nagaland. She loves cooking, travelling, reading and spending time with her children.

IRIS YINGZEN is an Associate Professor in the Department of History, at Sao Chang College in Tuensang, Nagaland. Her areas of concern are Northeast India, sustainable arts, place and identity. She is a self-taught artist who works with acrylics on hand-woven nettle fibre textiles and indigo-dyed cotton. Her work has been featured in *Himal Southasian*, National Folklife, Hutton Lectures, and North East Social Research

Centre (NESRC) Monograph Series. Her recent exhibition was at the international conference, Locating Northeast India: Human Mobility, Resource Flows and Spatial Linkages, held at Tezpur University, Assam in 2018.

JUNGMAYANGLA LONGKUMER is a Professor in the Department of Agricultural Extension, Nagaland University, SASRD, Medziphema Campus. She has published three books: *Change & Continuity in Tribal Villages: A Sociological Study (*2009), *Pottery: Earth Stories* (2010), *Gift in the Pot: Earth Poetry* (2014).

KUTOLI N holds a Masters degree in East Asian Studies and a Master of Philosophy in Japanese Studies from the University of Delhi. Apart from writing, she once ran a small crochet business-kotori, and occasionally deals in pashmina. At present she is self-learning free-hand watercolour art, and has just published a devotional book.

LICCA KIHO is twenty-one years old and is from Kohima. She is currently doing a Masters in Museology at Calcutta University. She chose Museology because art inspires her and she dreams of becoming an art curator in a museum. She became interested in the world of art in high school and began working with watercolours. Inspired by anime, she got into animation drawing and later experimented with poster colours and in her second year at college, learnt about abstract art and that became her style. Her paintings were first displayed in 2017 in Nagaland. Later, at a mini art exhibition she sold her first painting and today, with some help from her friends, she gets orders for paintings and manages to earn something as a struggling artist.

LIMATOLA LONGKUMER is a self-taught artist who likes working with micron pen and watercolour. She believes in intricacy of design yet loves minimalism. Her work is mostly monochrome and is influenced by the delicate lines in a woman's body.

MANENJUNGLA AIER is a twenty-two year old freelance artist from Nagaland. She has a Bachelors degree in English and is currently working in a Dimapur-based NGO called Serendip Guardians that deals with mental health awareness.

MARIANNE MURRY's real name is R. Mhonlumi Murry although most people know her by her artistic name Marianne. She graduated from Japfu Christian College in 2018 and is a self-taught artist. She began drawing at the age of ten, inspired by various artists whose wonderful work motivated her to draw more and improve her skills. She wants to make art her profession although as the eldest in her family she may have to think of other alternatives to support her family. Currently, she has no plans to go to university but is keen to explore doing something that will align with her interests and help her achieve her goals.

MOASO AIER is a contemporary realist artist. She has been painting with oils for the past fifteen years. Her work is primarily figurative with a nouveau element to it. Moaso is a member of the prestigious International Guild of Realism. She has participated in several art shows both nationally and internationally with good success.

NAROLA CHANGKIJA lives in Australia and teaches creative writing at Griffith University, Queensland. She is interested in the storytelling format of the graphic novel, and in the folklore and tales of the Naga tribes of North-Eastern India. Her 2008 PhD submission at Griffith University was a graphic novel script based on the myth of the tiger-soul.

NEIKEHIENUO MEPFHÜO is from Kohima, Nagaland. She has done her PhD in Comparative Literature on the subject of a comparative study of Naga and Native American Tribal Literature. She currently teaches Functional English at Kohima College, Kohima.

NINI LUNGALANG, 70 years old, is a teacher who believes language is the most powerful gift bestowed on mankind. According to her, every word, apart from its obvious lexical meaning, has a worth, a weight, an implictness of its own. For her, it is delving into this mysterious realm that makes reading, teaching and writing so exciting and rewarding. She believes writing is a search for truth in oneself, however painful it may be. All art, for her, is honest. She loves music, for it touches the spirit when reason fails. She loves people – 'the good, the bad, the ugly; – and believes that each person is precious. She also loves dogs because they love you back unconditionally, they never lie and, best of all, they don't snit back at you.

PHEJIN KONYAK: In between writing and running her farm 'The Konyak Tea Retreat', Phejin Konyak travels to remote villages to spend time with tribal elders to document the vanishing tattoo tradition of her tribe. She feels that it is important to preserve one's cultural heritage in order to keep identity intact. She has authored a book based on her research, *The Konyaks: Last of the Tattooed Headhunters* (2017).

RŌZUMARĪ SAMSĀRA (born Rosemary Kikon, in Kohima, Nagaland) graduated from Delhi University, Hong Kong University of Science & Technology and Ruhr-Universität Bochum, Germany. She worked with several NGOs and INGOs but in her midlife her destiny ferried her to Copenhagen where she studied physical theatre at The Commedia School; and she recycled herself into a poet, performer and an inter-disciplinary artist with a unique Northeast-Indian-Female-Tribal flair.

SIRAWON TULISEN KHATHING is a visual designer, illustrator and co-founder of Biscoot & Rain, a creative company. Her work is largely inspired by her home town, cultures, histories and lifestyle of North East India. Her professional career has involved working in design and publishing in Bombay and Bangalore. Having grown up away from home for schooling and work has fostered in her a yearning for her roots, culture, traditions and history. Sira was born in Shillong, Meghalaya and is currently based in Dimapur, Nagaland, learning and researching local products, sustainable alternatives, collaborating with artists and designing for a letterpress studio.

METONGLA AIER is Sira's grandmother (Azao), 95 years old, healthy and active.

TALILULA is a researcher from Nagaland with an interest in exploring folk traditions and beliefs. She has previously worked on Ao-Naga proverbs and *Wawa Menü*, a comic tradition that is practised within the Ao community. Currently a content editor for *Nagaland Today*, she also writes fiction and poetry. Based in Dimapur, she shares custody of a cat with her sister.

TEMSULA AO published her first book of poems in 1988 and till date has six poetry books to her credit. Her other books include one on her own culture *The Ao-Naga Oral Tradition* (1988/reprinted 2013), *Henry James and the Search for an Ideal Heroine* (1989), *These Hills Called Home: stories from a war zone* (Zubaan-Penguin, 2006), *Laburnum for my Head* (2009), her memoir *Once Upon A Life* (Zubaan, 2013), the collected volume of poetry *Book of Songs* 2013), the collected volume of essays on her culture *On Being A Naga* (2014), and her first novel *Aosenla's Story* (Zubaan, 2017). Ao is the recipient of the Padma Sri for Literature and Education (2007), The Nagaland Governor's Award for Distinction in Literature (2009), The Sahitya Academy Award for English (2013), The Kusumagraj National Literature Award (2015). She is the first Naga woman to obtain PhD (1983), the first Naga to become a Professor in a central university (1989) and her works have been translated into Assamese, Bengali, Hindi, Kannada and German and her works are in the syllabi of colleges and universities around the country including Nagaland University, Kohima. She recently completed her tenure as Chairperson, Nagaland State Commission for Women based in Theje Home.

THEJAKHRIENUO YHOME, a.k.a. ThejYhome is a twenty-five year old self-taught artist from Kohima, Nagaland. She holds a degree in Animation and VFX. Those who've met her might say she is mind numbingly invested in the knowledge of all things geek. Her art and storytelling are heavily influenced by both Western and Japanese comics, animated shows, movies, and video games. She is currently working as a production designer in Bangalore, creating character and asset designs for animated TV shows. She frequently dabbles in concept design, illustration and comic book work for freelance and personal projects.

T. KEDITSU is a poet, writer and educator. She is co-founder of the Centre for Indigenous Knowledge & Alternative Learning (CIKAL) and advocates the revival of Indigenous Naga textiles and women's narratives through her popular Instagram avatar @mekhalamama. She currently teaches in Kohima College, Kohima.

VISHÜ RITA KROCHA is the author of a poetry book *A Bucket of Rain*, a Naga folktale book for children *Shoposho*, and is co-author of the poetry book *Echoes of Spring*. A journalist by profession, she has worked as a newspaper columnist and correspondent for the Nagaland-based English daily *Eastern Mirror* for over five years. In November 2013, she founded PenThrill, a small home-based publication house. She currently writes for Nagaland-based English daily, *The Morung Express*.

Glossary

Abao: Father. Changki dialect, Ao-Naga language.

Achep: West. Changki dialect, Ao-Naga language.

Ajen: East. Changki dialect, Ao-Naga language.

Alao: Mother. Changki dialect, Ao-Naga language, used only for the Longchari clan women.

Alar: Slaves. Ao-Naga, language.

Aling: Bamboo string. Changki dialect, Ao-Naga language.

Angu pongsen: Fish steamed with bamboo-shoot and wild greens in a cylinder of bamboo, which is kept near an open fire to heat up and cook the fish curry. Chungli dialect, Ao-Naga language.

Arre/Aya/Ayah: Commonly used in various ways to express a variety of inexpressible feelings.

Azao: Grandmother. Changki dialect, Ao-Naga language.

Chachem:	Packed food wrapped in a leaf, consisting of rice, meat and chutney. Changki dialect, Ao-Naga Language.
Chepralikla:	'One who wears a shell'. Archaic Ao-Naga language.
Chungliyimti:	Ancient settlement of Naga people, presently a village in Tuensang district, Nagaland.
Gaonbura:	Village elder. Borrowed from the Assamese language.
Khel:	Locality. Borrowed from the Assamese language.
Khui:	Betel nut, eaten with betel leaf and slaked lime. Changki dialect, Ao-Naga.
Luhatina:	Metal scrap. Commonly used term, borrowed from the Assamese language.
Machang:	An open verandah on bamboo stilts that is usually attached to the main house. Commonly used term.
Meyutsüngba:	God of the Land of the Dead. Chungli dialect of the Ao-Naga language.
Mistris:	Carpenters/masons. Borrowed from the Assamese language.
Nagamese:	Pidgin Assamese which has become the lingua franca in Nagaland.
Ngupde:	Also referred to as Napti, Leiang, unknown origin.
Oja:	Mother. Chungli dialect, Ao-Naga language.

Oki tssoa: 'Building a house'. Lotha-Naga language.

Otsüla: Grandmother. Chungli dialect, Ao-Naga language.

Paan: Combination of betel nut, betel leaf, slaked lime and an assortment of fillings, consumed widely around the country.

Phika cha: Black tea. Borrowed from the Assamese language.

Player-boots: Costly branded football boots; commonly used term in villages in Zunheboto district, Nagaland.

Thu bao: Large hand-woven bamboo baskets used for storing grain. Zhavame village dialect, Chakhesang-Naga language.

Rumini: Hand-woven woman's cloth, white cotton with two thin lines of color (black and coral pink), worn with a matching white shawl. Chakhesang-Naga.

Tsukden: Storage place above the fireplace for firewood. Chungli dialect, Ao-Naga language.

Tsumar: Plains-person. Chungli dialect, Ao-Naga language.

Tsüngsa: Bamboo platform, similar to machang. Lotha-Naga language.

Yanpi: 'Knit the village'. Lotha-Naga language.

Yisu: Jesus. Ao-Naga language.